Sing,
RONNIE,
BLUE

All inquiries and permission requests should be addressed to the Publisher, Rager Media, 1016 West Abbey, Medina, Ohio 44265.
First edition 2007
11   10   09   08   07   5   4   3   2   1

ISBN 978-0-9792091-7-8

Manufactured in the United States of America.
The paper used in this publication meets the minimum requirements of American National Standard for Information Sciences—Permanence of Paper for Printed Library Materials, ANSI Z39.48—1984.∞

Cover image: "Cloudburst," copyright © 2007 by John D. Morrison, www.prairievistas.com
Cover Design: Amy Freels
Interior Design: C Sutherland Graphic Designs

None of the characters or institutions appearing in this novel exist outside its pages. *Sing Ronnie Blue* is entirely a work of fiction.

Sing, RONNIE BLUE

Gary D. Wilson

for Modena,
Christopher,
Nicholas

Sing, RONNIE BLUE

*H*e is dreaming of machines, either disassembled already or coming apart in dark space. Gears and rods, wheels, bearings, a fender from a 1939 Chevy coupe, armatures, dials, switches, valves and a lone white kitchen clock, hands frozen at eleven, trailing cogs and pins and springs like a comet's tail. He can feel himself groping for the parts in slow motion. He wants to gather them in, put them back together, but they are always just beyond reach, and there is no pedal or lever or button to stop whatever he is on. Like a love boat in a tunnel, a tunnel without walls, without water, whoo-shoo, whoo-shoo, whoo-shoo, whoo-shoo echoing in the distance, a pump sucking air, a compressor, a grease gun beating at a zerk that won't fill. At the edge of his vision a mannequin bobs and weaves, arms, legs, head detached from the torso, smeared red. No hair, no ears, a mouth closed, a nose, eye sockets. The mouth opens. Dark, as if it has swallowed the darkness around it.

1

*R*onnie Blue wakes up hungry. All he can think of is peanut butter. Maybe he's hungry every night, but doesn't know it since he sleeps through it. Like Charlene now. She has no idea of his hunger or his dream. She's off in some never-never land herself, one he can't get to without rousing her. And if he does that, she won't be there, she'll be here—and mad because he woke her. He wonders who she's with but decides he really doesn't want to know and flops to his back, staring at the amber glow from a streetlight on the bedroom ceiling.

His body tenses as a semi, engine lugging up an overpass on the interstate three blocks away, tops the incline and the driver opens it up on the way down. Grinning, he imagines the chase. Flashing lights, sirens, the smell of hot motors. A maverick trucker hauling hijacked goods, a badass cop in fast pursuit. And they have to shoot it out, guns blazing, blistering white against the insides of his eyelids.

The bed bounces as he gets up, and she rolls toward where he was lying, then away, as if repelled by the warmth. She is uncovered, naked, the tangled sheet hanging limp over the foot of the bed, her back to him, left leg cocked like a runner's. She is seventeen. He has known her for a year and a half and has watched her hips and breasts swell, her waist pinch, her face become more womanly and worried. She is not beautiful, and she is no longer cute, but she likes him, even on occasion still says she loves him.

He met her, just like in the movies, at the McDonald's on West Kellogg in Wichita. She was working the counter and he told her she should be in that TV commercial where the girl says, "We do it all for you." She looked at him, smiling in a way that made his groin tingle. There was no mistaking her meaning when she said, "And we do, too." Over the next week he ate lunch there every day—it was only a block from the Amoco station where he worked then—and every day they got a little friendlier, a little bolder, until he asked her out for Friday night. To the movies. She loved the movies. They picked up some chips and nuts and a six pack, and she told him to park in the third row from the back fence. In the last row you got hassled all the time, but here they weren't as likely to be bothered. He asked her how she knew and she smiled again. He wondered what Ronald McDonald would think if he could see her.

They sat in the back seat, front seats folded down for their feet, and ate and sipped beer. Halfway through the movie, as the crazy was about to make another kill, she scooted over against him, shorts tightening between her legs. His arm went around her and she lifted her knee over his, his hand catching the back of her thigh. She pressed closer, kissed him. When he slid his finger under the elastic of her panties, she bit his ear and yanked his belt loose. He pulled her shorts and underwear down her legs, and she straddled his lap. And just sat, for what seemed forever. Settled, hugging him, head sideways on his shoulder. Through her hair, he could see the crazy at a woman's bedroom window, and as the music grew more sinister and the beat quickened, so did Charlene. Swiveling bone on bone, gyrating up and down around, up and down around, breath hot on his neck, a gasp, a whimper, the shadow of a man with a raised axe falling across the woman's bed, her look of horror as she realized what was about to happen, a scream, terrible and climactic.

His stomach growls as he stares at the slope of her hip, the downy hollow in the small of her back. He could take her now from the rear, just where she is. Or from the front, or the top, or the side, anywhere he wants. Because she'll let him. Because it's him, Ronnie Blue, doing it. But that's no good, laying the old lady because there's nothing else to do, so you won't have to think of anything else. He's not that bad off yet. He still has a brain. He can still figure a way.

But he needs to come up with something fast. He hasn't worked in almost six weeks now, and he's down to his last twenty. Enough for some gas and a couple of hamburgers, and that's it. That's all. No more movies, no more records. She's been complaining already that they never do anything but hang around and watch TV. He tells her she can always go home if it gets too bad. But he knows she won't, not for any longer than she just has to.

Her daddy was killed when she was ten—a backhoe turned over on him—and since then her mother has spent most of her days waitressing and her nights entertaining cowboys. The rougher riding the better, she says. And sometimes when Charlene's home, the cowboys make passes at her, too. It wouldn't be so bad if they knew when to stop, but they don't. Once a guy came into the bathroom while her mother was outside, pulled open the shower curtain and stood there staring at her, turned on but scared enough he didn't do anything. Another time she woke up in the morning with her mother's boyfriend asleep on the floor beside her bed. Her mother never says much when it happens, tries to joke about it or whatever. But let it be him, Ronnie Blue, and then it's something else. Like the night he stayed over late with Charlene and her mother came home around three and found them. All hell broke loose, and they were just making out. Nothing heavy. They even had their clothes on. But you would have thought from hearing her mother that he was holding a knife to Charlene's throat. One minute she's a slut and the next a virgin princess. In be-tween she might as well not exist. So she's never going to run off and live with mama again, and he wouldn't move in there for love nor money. No, sir, he has enough to worry about without that.

The worst part is, none of it needed to be. None of it had to happen. If Carl had only kept his mouth shut, the crippled old fart, and not come out to the garage that day, there wouldn't be a problem. He would still have a job, money, a little peace of mind, which doesn't seem to be asking so godalmighty much.

He did, though. He came out. Ronnie could hear the clank and creak of his crutches and leg braces before he ever got to the door. They're the kind of crutches you put your arms through and lean on while you drag your legs up under you again. Creak-scrape, creak-scrape, creak-scrape. Only that day it sounded different. Slower, more deliberate. He knew something was up.

"Ronnieblue." Carl always said his full name, as if it were one word. "We've got ourselves a heap of trouble."

The car he was lubricating was on the lift, but he still had to stoop a little to stand under it, so all he could see of Carl were braces and crutches from the waist down. And those immaculate shoes, never a smudge or scuff, pointing straight at him. He wondered if people with crippled hands kept their nails as perfectly. One thing about Carl— even now he'd have to say it—he didn't give up after his wreck. He didn't just sit down and die. He moved, and then moved some more, even when it hurt. And he grimaced and swore and took what Ronnie felt were too many pills. But he didn't quit. In fact, Ronnie thought he was plain foolish sometimes, like the nights after nine when the place went self-service and Carl ran it alone. Why, he was a regular sitting duck in that office, not being able to get around any better than he could. But that's his business now. To hell with him.

"You're positive—there's no doubt in your mind—that you put the oil plug back in Mrs. Brandt's car?"

"I already told you," the nozzle of the grease gun aimed at the floor.

"Well, she says you didn't and that's why her engine burned up on the way to Oklahoma City."

"She's an old bag."

"But a rich one, who can afford all the lawyers she wants."

"Let her."

"She's serious, boy."

"So am I."

"She wants a new car."

"Who doesn't?"

Carl's feet rose, toes dangling like a puppet's, as he shifted his weight. "I don't think you understand what I'm saying."

"No, now that's not true. It's just that I don't *like* what you're saying, because I didn't do anything wrong and you're trying to tell me I did. But you got no reason to. I'm the best person you've ever had here. Or ever will, and you know it. I don't get sick, I work hard, I'm not sloppy. You could eat your supper off this floor right now. Just the way you said to keep it so there wouldn't be no accidents. And if you ever need extra help, who comes in? Me, ain't that right? No complaining. I just do my job—and good, too. But now you're taking a worry-wart old flea bag woman's word over mine because she has money?"

"Something happened, Ronnieblue. There wasn't a drop of oil in that motor."

"Could have been a lot of things."

"But it looks awful much like a plug and you know it."

"You're saying I left it out?"

"Or maybe at least didn't get it tightened down."

"And that's it? That's all you've got to say?"

Carl shrugged.

Ronnie Blue yanked free another arm's length of hose and stepped out from under the car, grease gun in hand. "Okay. I got it figured now. I see what you're up to. What you're really planning to do is tell them lawyers it was me, dumb old me, ain't you, and if they want to settle up with somebody, I'm the one. Ain't that it?" He pulled the hose out as far as it would go.

"I don't know if I'd say that exactly."

"You don't, do you?" He pumped a pound of grease between Carl's feet, and before he could move squirted another mound around the base of each crutch. "What, then, Carl? Because that's what it sounds like. It sounds like you're calling me a liar and want to use me to get yourself off the hook. And I don't like that. Not one bit."

"Now wait a minute here. What're you—" He was sweating, even though it wasn't hot, turning one way, the other, as he followed the course of the grease gun laying a perfect ridge of lubricant around him in an ever-widening spiral.

"You're crazy, Ronnieblue. One mean, crazy son of a bitch."

He had to say something, Ronnie knew that, because he was scared. You could smell it on him, like urine you squeeze out when you don't really have to go but do anyway.

The thought of Carl peeing his pants made him laugh. He kept on laughing as he counted from the cash register the hundred dollars due him. And he was laughing yet when he started his car and burned rubber toward the grease rack—just to be sure Carl moved.

He opens the refrigerator. It smells cold and dry. Slightly musty with the hint of old food. There are two Cokes, a bowl of leftover macaroni and cheese, a chunk of Velveeta darkening around the edges, a shriveled slice of pizza, one limp carrot and a margarine dish full of brownie crumbs.

Maybe he shouldn't have done it, Carl being crippled and all. But he did come out there to fire him, that was plain enough. Carl just didn't trust him anymore, and he couldn't work for somebody who felt like that, no matter what. Besides, it was funny. Even now the picture of Carl trying to get out of the way without landing on his ass makes him smile. He'd do it again just for that.

At the kitchen table he munches nuts and burned edges from the brownie dish and drinks a Coke, the fizz and crunch filling the inside of his head. If Carl would only have backed off, damn him. But he wouldn't. Maybe pride does go before a fall.

No, he's thought about it and decided what he really wants is a place of his own. His own garage where he can do what he does better than anybody—which is fix cars—and do it without any hassle. No Carls—and no fathers, either, telling him to junk the goddamn motor like he said, not repair it, and if he can't do that just to get on out and mow goddamn lawns or something. No, sir. No more of that. With a place of his own he can tell them all to take a flying leap, because he'll be raking in dough so fast he won't even be able to keep track of it. He won't have to worry about rent or food or any of the rest, and when Charlene says she wants to go to the movies or buy some records or new clothes, fine. But they have to have money to get started. For that they have to think beyond McDonald's. They have to dream a little, make some plans, be willing to take a few chances.

He leans back, peering out the window. First light has risen in the crack between cloud cover and horizon. As far as he can see, a thin pink line is broken here and there by stark silhouettes of trees and buildings. Liquid light pours in under clouds, rippled as a sand bar, ever brighter, more vivid, purple, rose, gold, the molten white rim of the sun itself flooding the room with dawn.

In the distance, he hears muffled popping and cracking sounds, some closer, more distinct, like rubber bands snapping on paper. Then it's quiet but for the roar of an engine, coming, he judges, from near the end of the street. Tires scream to life and Ronnie Blue knows who it is. Martin Zimmerman. The crazy bastard must be doing fifty by the time he passes the front of the house and opens his dumps, windows rattling, floor rumbling, a godawful screech as he rounds the corner on his way to the interstate, the packet of firecrackers he threw exploding on the doorstep with the clackety-clack stutter of a machine gun.

"Ronnie?" Charlene runs from the hallway holding his t-shirt to her front. "My god, Ronnie, what was that?"

"Zimmerman saying happy birthday."

"What?"

"You know, happy birthday, Ronnie Blue, and the good old U. S. of A., too? It's the Fourth, dense-head. Of Ju-ly."

"What time is it?"

"I don't know. Five, five-thirty, why?"

"He's going to end up having his party in jail." She pulls the t-shirt on over her head.

"Zimmerman? They have to catch him first. And that ain't likely."

"They can do most anything they want to when they set their minds to it."

"What've you got against Zimmerman, anyway?"

"Nothing."

"Then why're you always on him?"

"I'm not."

"Are, too."

"Come on, Ronnie. I ain't even had a cigarette yet."

"And you shouldn't, either. Those things'll kill you."

"Jesus, what's your problem?" she whines.

"Go on, if you have to. Get them. And clean up your mouth while you're at it."

He watches the wag of her hips, the muscles smoothing her legs as she goes to the bedroom. And coming back, the jiggly lines her nipples make on the shirt.

"You know the real reason he does stuff like that, don't you?" he says, brushing paper wads off the front step so they can sit down. "He wants your body."

"Well, that's sure a weird way of showing it."

"I told him I'd pound his ass if he touched you."

"God, you're tough," her voice smiling.

"I mean it. And the same goes for you."

"I'm so scared I can't stop shaking." She flicks ashes into the yard.

"I would be if I was you. But you can suit yourself."

"You're really on it this morning, ain't you?"

"What?"

"Turn twenty-three and you're ready to whip the world."

"All I said was if you messed around."

"But nobody is."

"Better not, either."

"Okay, Ronnie. Let's just drop it now, okay?"

He locks his arms around his knees and, chin resting on top of them, stares out at the street.

"See," she says, "now you're in one of your pissy moods again. I can't figure you at all sometimes. I mean, one minute you're fine, then *bam* you're acting like this."

"I can't help it."

"That ain't no excuse."

"I can't. My mama said she heard fireworks when I was born, and there's been fireworks ever since. Me and the good old U. S. of A. But them sparks ain't been all bad, have they? I mean, I can still light you up."

"Ron-nie!" pushing his hand from her leg. "I ain't even awake yet."

"Sure, sure."

"Maybe later."

"Be too hot then."

"We can go someplace cool," she says.

"Where, Mama's? Crawl in with her and her boyfriend? She-it!"

"No, I was thinking of the public library, dummy."

"One thing we ain't going to do," he says, standing, nose twitching at the smell of asphalt rising on the hot air. "We ain't going to sit around here all day eating each other alive. To hell with that."

"Well? You got an idea, or are you just sounding off again?"

"How much money you have?"

"Some, why?"

"It's my birthday and we're going to celebrate it, that's why. We're going to live it up till we can't go no more. We're going to eat and drink and play, then start in all over again till we're sick of it, till you're begging me to stop."

She grins, eyes sparkling. It excites her when he talks that way, and he knows she'll go anywhere with him now, do anything he wants, because it's him, Ronnie Blue, talking, saying what is and what isn't. It's him, Ronnie Blue, about to set the world on fire and her with it.

"Now get along, get ready," he says, pulling her up and swatting her backside on the way in. "The junkman's son is going home, and he's taking his woman with him."

She stops, glances back, as if to see whether he's serious.

"That's right. Lord willing and the creek don't rise, we're heading home. For the time of your life."

2

John Klein parks parallel to the curb and steps up to the door of the bank. Shielding his eyes, he peers in past the customer's counter with ends of forms hanging like wilted white peonies over the tops of their slots, past the row of tellers' windows redone in natural oak and now flecked with color from the single stained glass window high on the east wall, past the black-topped desks cleared of work for the holiday, directly to the heart of the matter—the heavy steel door of the vault faintly gleaming in the far reaches of the room.

All is well. As it should be, as he expects it will be every time he puts his face to the glass.

He turns away smiling, thinking how much he would have argued with anyone who would have told him when he left Bartlett's Junction five years ago, presumably for good, that he would one day be back, standing where his father, his grandfather and his great-grandfather before him had stood gazing into the bank as they had, not because it made any difference, but because they had also done it and he was afraid—almost superstitiously afraid—to break the ritual.

He'd not been back in town more than six months when he woke up just before sunrise one morning and, seized by a compulsion the likes of which he'd never experienced, drove to the bank. Coming down Main from the north, he met his father rounding the corner of First Street from the east. Neither said a word to the other, merely nodded, peered through the bank windows, nodded again as they got back into their cars. But it was clear how proud his father was, how good he felt seeing his son there, the business thus beginning to pass as surely as baldness to the fourth generation of Kleins.

He had certainly never planned on a banking career. As a child, it embarrassed him that his father charged people interest on money he loaned them. In Bartlett's Junction, you didn't get a loan from the bank, you got it from Bud Klein; and to make friends repay more than they had borrowed seemed to John Klein's young mind unfair, and at times, immoral.

The first real fight he ever got into was with Obie Dillon. They were in the sandbox at school, which was located in a recessed area at the southeast corner of the old building, nubby dark limestone walls rising on two sides, a black metal fire escape just out of reach above their heads. The sand was grey, as were the boards containing it, and the place was constantly shaded, due, he now knows, to the hour of their recess period rather than to any metaphysical cause. But he still remembers it as a gloomy, cheerless place, perfect for generating quarrels.

Until their fight, he and Obie had been friends. Probably best friends. Obie's father was a carpenter and had built him a wonderful back yard playhouse. The two boys, living only a block apart, spent hours there, and once inside the playhouse, what Bud Klein and Jack Dillon did or said meant nothing to them.

But in the sandbox that day they had no such protection when Obie blurted, as though repeating breakfast conversation, "Your dad's a shit!"

He didn't answer. He couldn't.

Obie said it again, more loudly.

He felt hurt and angry and sick inside, like he was going to vomit.

"He's a shithead. He don't care about anybody but himself. A shithead," Obie said, pushing him toward the corner.

Planting his feet, he said half-heartedly: "Yeah? Says who?"

"Says me."

"Says you?"

"Yeah, me. What are you going to do about it?"

The words sounded strange coming from Obie's mouth. Like he wasn't used to them. Like they were uncomfortable, the way new shoes are the first couple of times you wear them.

He smiled then and reached out to touch Obie.

Obie knocked his hand away, and they dropped to the sand, pounding each other on the back, clawing, ripping clothes, pulling hair. Crying, because it really wasn't them fighting. It was their fathers.

And it didn't get any better the older he became. In fact, it got worse, as he felt more and more separated from his peers because of who he was. The easiest thing would have been for him to hang around with Doc Morgan's boy or Bob Yost, the lawyer's son, but he really had little other than class in common with them. They were three-letter jocks and considered themselves great lovers. He tended at that time more toward tennis and occasional dates. He was studious and enjoyed acting, painting and reading. A more solitary than social person.

His best—and only—friend during that period was Jay Benton, the Methodist minister's son, who had seemed to be going through the same thing himself. They understood each other. There was no need to talk about the problem unless they wanted to, and a couple of times they did, staying up late, trying to figure out why everyone else couldn't see things as clearly as they could. But usually what they did was go to Herman's on Saturday morning to shoot snooker, then maybe take a walk down the Santa Fe tracks to Miller's Hill or Watkins' Dam. During warm weather, if they were out after supper they might sneak over the fence to swim in old man Polk's pool, or sit on the curb pitching pebbles into the street in front of the laundromat. They had fun just doing what they were doing, nothing else mattering much, and they probably would have become life-long friends if Jay's dad hadn't been transferred to a larger church near Wichita.

And there he was, left sitting alone again. It wasn't anything new, so he wasn't exactly angry. Disappointed, frustrated, more tired than anything. Tired of not being what everyone seemed to expect him to be. Tired of always finding himself on the outside looking for a way in. Things were bad enough that when the opportunity came his junior year in high school for him to say to hell with it, he was ready.

Ronnie Blue could sing like nobody he'd ever heard. He was a natural tenor, by far the best in chorus. At times John Klein would stop singing himself to listen. The guy was so good he could have become a professional. But he didn't care. Even later, after they'd formed a duet and sang at club meetings and parties, it was hard to get Ronnie to rehearse. If he enjoyed something, he just did it. No big deal. Ten minutes before a performance was enough for him. "Let's go, man. I'm here now and I got music in my soul. We're going to knock their socks off." And once they had, he was finished until the next time.

The only thing he seemed to take seriously was his car. In those days, almost everybody had one. But his wasn't some leftover family sedan, maroon with an automatic transmission, that you had to look hard at to see whether your friend or his dad was driving. No way. Ronnie Blue's was a silver customized '58 Chevy Impala convertible that glittered and thundered and turned everyone's head. Like it or not, you noticed that car and you noticed who was in it.

"Did I see you with that Blue boy again?" John Klein's father asked one evening.

"When?"

"This afternoon."

"Maybe. Why?"

"You two seem to be spending a lot of time together."

"We have to practice, you know."

"I don't mean that. Your singing is nice. It's fine."

"The only other thing we do is ride around once in a while."

"But what about your other friends?"

"I don't have any."

"My point exactly. You need to make some so you can be with all different kinds of people and not just—"

"You mean I should sing with Ronnie Blue but not have him for a friend? Is that it?"

"Your mother and I just don't think he's what you might call the most . . . most . . ."

"Wholesome?"

"Well, all right, yes. He's not the most wholesome person you could be spending your time with."

"He's okay. He just does crazy things sometimes."

"Flushing a cherry bomb down the toilet at school wasn't just crazy. That could have cost a lot of money."

"But it didn't and nobody got hurt, right? It just upset a lot of people, that's all. A bunch of old—"

"That's another thing," his father's finger driving his words. "I for one don't like the way you've been talking lately."

"What do you mean?"

"That smart-aleky, sassy, dirty mouth of yours is what I mean, young man."

"Everybody from the junkyard talks that way, don't you know?"

"That has nothing to do with this."

"Does, too. Ronnie's dad owns a junkyard. That's really why you can't stand him, isn't it? Isn't it?"

"No, and I don't think—"

"Junkyard, junkyard, junkyard."

"John? Now listen to me, John."

"JUNKYARD!"

His father was right, of course. His friendship with Ronnie Blue could never last, not in a place like Bartlett's Junction. Or maybe anywhere else, for that matter. Only in that great, sustained adolescent present could they do as they pleased with no problems. The day John Klein announced where he was going to college, the end became visible.

"And how about you?" he asked Ronnie Blue. "What are you thinking about doing?"

They were heading north of town on a county road so full of dips and patches only the center was safe to drive on. Ronnie Blue was hunched over the wheel, lying on it, chin resting on his hands. He shook his head, shaggy blond hair flopping back and forth across the profile of his face.

"I don't know. I really don't know."

He straightened his arms against the wheel. The car rumbled and surged.

"How about the army? You thought about that?" He watched Ronnie Blue's eyes, shiny as washers, so clear and grey it was impossible to tell what he was thinking. "Or maybe technical school. They have some good courses in mechanics."

"So what are you, a goddamn counselor or something?"

"No, I—"

"That's all I hear out of old man Frye, too. Do this, do that. I keep telling him to bug off, but he won't let me alone. I'll do whatever I do, that's all. I can take care of myself."

It was starting to get dark. Winter dark that closes in on the inside of you, too, and brings the cold with it.

"I mean, I don't need no army. Get my ass shot off, what are you talking about? And I don't need no technical school. I can already fix any motor anywhere, anytime. Cars, trucks, tractors—makes no difference to me. And I don't need nobody to tell me how to do it. I know more than they do already. I ought to teach them. I'm a natural. It's a god-given gift. I mean, I don't need *nobody*! You hear? I don't—Shit!"

The car bottomed out over a small bridge, headlights suddenly lost in the dusk, coming down again in a flash across prickly, leafless hedge trees.

"One of these days I'm going to bust an axle on that bridge, and then they better watch out, because I'll fix those sons of bitches. I'll fix them good."

They were doing eighty-five, the wind sucking at the canvas top, the road a meaningless narrow band that kept unwinding toward them from some invisible point beyond the headlights.

Ronnie Blue turned on the radio, KFDI country twanging, beating at them, pleading. Mercury vapor yard lights blinked on here and there, scenes of frame houses and outbuildings, groves of trees frozen in the darkness, the smell of warm, wet manure wafting over them.

"You got any money?" Ronnie Blue said.

"Some. Why?"

"Enough to get drunk and laid?"

"What?"

"You heard me."

He was smiling now. But it was a strange smile, one that told John Klein it wasn't the time to talk. He could usually reason with Ronnie, bring him around to his way of thinking, make him laugh off the bad mood. But not now. Something was different about the way he had locked himself behind the wheel, eyes fixed on the road as if not really seeing it, lips pulled back, teeth glimmering in the green dash lights.

"How much will it take?"

"Fifty, sixty bucks. If we're not too particular."

"I guess I can handle that."

The grin and steely eyes turned on him.

"You bankers."

"I got paid today."

"You always have a little tucked away, don't you? Just in case."

"Listen, I worked my butt off for this, the same way you do for yours. Sixty hours this month putting up with old Bucko at the Co-op. So don't give me any shit, huh? It's here if we want it. If we don't, forget it. I could use the sleep."

They turned east on Highway 56 toward Marion. Four semis and a pickup, tagging each other in an elephantine line, erupted from the darkness at the top of a hill, roaring and clanging past, lights jiggling, the smell of rubber and diesel exhaust following like an unseen tail. Then the road was Ronnie Blue's again, and he opened it up until they approached the last set of curves before the river at the west edge of town.

"You ever had one?" Ronnie asked as their tires buzzed across the bridge.

"One what?"

"A whore."

"Sure, last night," John Klein said.

"I mean a real one."

He slugged Ronnie Blue on the shoulder and they laughed and everything seemed all right again.

The liquor store was in the middle of town, a half block down a dark side street, a single rusty sign with a shaded light over it announcing: BAUER'S LIQUORS. Neon Coors and Miller High Life signs glowed in the windows, OPEN dangling by a string on the door. Inside, a double row of fluorescent lights ran the length of the room, bottles along either side of an aisle leading to the cooler at the back. The store was empty, the clerk concentrating on a black and white TV behind the counter.

"Perfect," Ronnie Blue said. "Now when you get in there, act like you know what you're doing. I can't go. I've been here before and they've got my number. But you shouldn't have any trouble. Tell the guy straight off, before he even sees you, that you want a fifth of Jack Daniels. If he gives you any hassle, don't say a thing. Just leave. We'll go someplace else."

The man was watching Dolly Parton and didn't look away at all until he made change, and then it was too late. He shook his head— "Damn kids"—and settled back onto his stool.

Once out of town, they opened the bottle and passed it back and forth.

"Eiooow!"

"Wheeeew!"

"Ahhhhhhhh!"

Then they sank into slow and lazy sipping, warmth spreading to fingers, toes, lips. The road crossed the Flint Hills, rather than following them, up and down, up and down, as if tracing the course of great earthen waves, and they fell easily into the rhythm of the land.

Again on the level, the highway paralleling the Santa Fe Railroad the last leg into Emporia, John Klein asked: "How do you know so much about whores anyway?"

"I just do. Trust me."

And he must have because he drove straight to the hotel, talked to the man at the desk, and was ushered, John Klein in tow, directly to the second floor.

She was cleaning blood-red nails when he went in, and he remembers, dreamlike, her teeth—incisors, canines, molars—all straight, as if they'd been filed, gum popping in her mouth, the bite of cheap perfume on her neck, skin dry and raspy as a turtle's. And then the slow, passive rocking motion, so similar to what he'd felt on the road he caught himself wondering, with a certain curiosity but lack of acute need, if he was ever going to arrive. But he did, and she got up, collected her nail file and his money and left. In the hallway, his whore passed Ronnie's whore, who nodded at the back of Ronnie's head and mumbled: "Trigger-happy little sumbitch."

The trip home was quiet, with only an occasional semi blowing past, and the radio. The whiskey high was retreating to a dull ache in the back of his head. His eyes burned, his mouth felt dry and pasty, and he began to worry already that his penis was going to turn black and drop off.

At the outskirts of Bartlett's Junction, he roused himself enough to say, "That was all right."

"Yeah, it was," Ronnie Blue nodded. "And it'll even be better once I get control of myself. But I'm telling you, a whore just does something to me no other woman can, and before I know it, whammo! it's over."

That seemed to be about how fast the rest of their senior year went. They were together more, almost constantly, doing more and more things, as if intensity might make up for the fact that by the end of the summer they would be separating.

They sang more—and better—a weekend seldom going by without a performance somewhere. The duet was one of the hardest things for either of them to give up, and their selections took on a sad, bittersweet tone. They drank more. Enough that Bud Klein said he was going to ground his son for the remainder of the school year if he kept on, and the tennis coach said he was going to kick him off the team. But he ignored them and continued doing whatever he felt like, reasonably sure that neither of them really wanted to carry out his threat. It would just be too much trouble for so little time.

Their final fling came on the next to last weekend John Klein was to be home. They began drinking early in the evening, and by sundown they were on their way to Miller's Hill with the Whitman twins, Jean and Jeanette. Before they were even past the tracks at the south edge of town, Ronnie Blue was holding up Jean's bra like a trophy.

At the hill, they stayed in the car a while, each couple out of sight of the other, but not out of range of the heavy breathing, smacking, giggling. Then they tumbled into the grass, running half-naked hand in hand up the hillside, their drunkenness allowing them an aura of carefree innocence in what they conceived to be the exercise of nature's dictates.

Afterward, they left for a swim at Watkins' Dam and there, he was sure, the girls switched on him and Ronnie. It would have been impossible to tell for certain, or to prove it if he'd had to, since they looked alike and wore identical outfits, including underclothes. And it didn't make any difference really, except that it felt funny. For the girls it was a lark, and he and Ronnie Blue had already shared everything else.

When they'd taken the girls home, they drove up Main Street, turned left on the highway, went under the underpass and west to the

Baitshop, made a U-turn and started back. Nothing was open, there were no cars in sight, no lights on in the houses.

Ronnie Blue floorboarded it. Tires screamed, the car fishtailed, and they catapulted down the highway, mufflers backing off like fireworks in the underpass. Killing his lights, he turned into the far drive of his father's junkyard.

They got out, finished drinking everything but a six pack of beer and hot-wired the old junker pickup Chester Blue used to tow wrecks in and out of the yard. It had no doors, no muffler, no windshield and no lights. But there was enough of a moon that Ronnie Blue could see what to run into. A '49 Ford coupe, a '75 Camaro, a '71 Volkswagen beetle. Forward and back, gears grinding, metal screeching, glass shattering. John Klein held onto the door frame with one hand, a beer with the other, whooping and yelling, scared and thrilled, but not for a moment wanting off the incredible wild beast he was riding.

Neither of them paid attention to the first shotgun blast, but the second splattered pellets too near to be ignored. Ronnie Blue popped the clutch to kill the motor.

"The old man. Come on. Keep down."

They ran to where junked appliances stood like blocks of salt in the moonlight.

"He won't come over here. He thinks the whole place is full of rats and mad dogs. Give me a beer."

They sat on top of a chest freezer, drinking, dangling their legs. It was John Klein who started singing. "All You Need Is Love," "Blowing in the Wind," "Mercedes Benz," "Bad, Bad Leroy Brown."

"Sing, damn you," poking Ronnie Blue in the ribs.

They stood on the freezer, running through all the numbers they'd ever done, arms locked around each other's waists, beers held triumphantly out toward the junkyard audience.

Exactly the position they were in when Dewey Cole trained the spotlight from his police car on them.

Chester Blue didn't press charges, but Bud Klein did have to come to the junkyard to pick up his son.

It was a cool week between him and his parents. Their leave-taking the next Sunday was more one of relief than sorrow. "Be careful," his mother and father said, nearly in unison, as if half-expecting never to see him again.

But sometime in the course of his years at college, he changed, and he did come back. Sporadically at first, weekends mainly. Then more regularly, spending the whole summer between his junior and senior years clerking at the bank.

And suddenly he was back for good, and he guesses he's glad, knows he is. Especially now with Linda there.

She came to town a year ago to fill in for one of the regular third grade teachers who was taking maternity leave. She wants to stay now, she tells him. She likes Bartlett's Junction, thinks it's a nice place to live, peaceful and quiet, a perfect town for raising a family.

He wants her to stay, too, and each morning after checking the bank, he drives out to Spruce Street to see if everything is in order at Mrs. Mayhew's, where Linda has an apartment on the second floor.

Her blinds are up. He waves, even though he knows she's probably showering, since in an hour he's coming to get her for breakfast at his parents' house, an ordeal he would just as soon forget, but feels bound to attend. Later, though, once they're free again, once they've made love in Linda's room and are relaxed and back in good humor, they'll go on a picnic—just the two of them—and then to the carnival and finally to the fireworks. So everything considered, it should be a decent day, one to look forward to rather than dread. He could, after all, be going everywhere alone, a notion which, because of her, he has come to find less and less tolerable.

He toots the horn, cringes, then laughs at himself. He steps on the gas, gravel drumming the fenders of the Thunderbird as he turns the corner.

Locust is the last street on the west side of town. Beyond it, corn rows and pastures and plowed wheat stubble stretch out toward far fence lines. At the north end of the street is a stop sign beside the Bait-shop, where Locust intersects Highway 50.

He waits there, watching an approaching car, judging its speed and distance. Not until it is nearly upon him does he recognize it. Still sleek and gleaming, the Chevy rumbles toward him, as if chewing the pavement before it. So odd. So strange, he feels childish and foolish.

Sunlight sparks from the car's windshield. He catches a glimpse of a woman, lean and harsh, yet young-looking beside Ronnie Blue, who is hunched against the wheel, smiling intently at something by the road.

Suddenly unsure of what he would say after five years, and whether he wants to say anything, John Klein drops the hand he was about to wave and glances at the field next to him, thinking how much they need rain.

3

The make and year of the car at the stop sign come to him automatically: 1978 Thunderbird. Show him a hundred rapid-fire and he can name them all. Flip-flip. Like flash cards in his mind. But that's all there is to it. He sees the car and it's gone, a momentary black blot at the edge of his vision.

What he is really concentrating on, what is making him smile, is the sign just before the county road going north—the Canada road, they call it, tongue in cheek, since it only goes to Canada, Kansas, fifteen miles away—the sign that reads: BARTLETT'S JUNCTION, POP. 2,157. The last two numbers are new, crisp black numerals on a white enamel square that is whiter than the dirty white, nearly beige, of the rest of the sign. More people, or fewer, it's hard to tell. AN ALL AMERICAN CITY—WITH PRIDE!

"Here we are," he says, elbowing Charlene.

She glances up at the white stucco Baitshop, the Budweiser sign over the front door rocking in the wind, then back at her thumbnail, raw and chewed to the quick.

"Can't you say *anything?*"

She shrugs.

"Come on, woman!"

She turns her head away.

Sulky bitch. She reminds him of her mother. She gets something in her head and that's it, you might as well forget anything else. He brought her here to have fun, but she's going to mess it up because she's going to get him in a bad mood after while, and then all hell's going to break loose. There's just too much to see and do, too many stories to tell for her to be pouting around all day.

He wants her to know about the underpass where he spent an hour one night hanging upside down on a rope painting RONNIE BLUE WAS HERE across the top of the wall. And it's still there. A little faded from exhaust, but there. One semi, a big-ass cattle truck, nearly got him. Couldn't have missed by more than six inches. She'd like that. She'd laugh if she'd listen.

And he wants to tell her about the Bartlett's Junction Motel on the other side of the underpass. *Deluxe Rooms, TV, Bath, Air—$8.95 Single* showing through a rusty, painted-over sign. Nobody has actually stayed there since he can remember, except for Josh Billings, a mean and cranky old man who at one time used the motel to sell what he said was antique furniture. He would line the veranda every morning with tables, chairs and couches, and every evening take them back in. A piece to a room, locking the doors behind him with keys he carried on a chain at his side like a jailor. One night he, Ronnie Blue, and a bunch of other guys snuck in the rear windows of the rooms and sat there on the chairs and couches, their faces painted like clowns, waiting for old Josh to open up. He damn near died.

That sort of thing. Or the car wash where they rigged the soap dispenser so that when you turned on the spray, the whole place filled with suds. They got a couple of people that way.

But it was all in fun. Hell, you had to do something. Otherwise you'd just wither up and blow away. Nobody'd even know you were gone if you didn't leave them something to remember.

They idle on past the Conoco station, the Standard-turned-Tex-aco station, the cut-rate, self-service station to the intersection where Main Street broadens and empties into the highway like a creek into a river.

He turns and settles back, hand on her thigh. He likes the way her leg feels through a cotton dress with no slip, the soft material sliding back and forth over warm skin.

She crosses her legs and hunches forward, gnawing the wounded thumb.

Moody bitch. Here she is, right in the middle of where he came from, like she's always talking about—"When're you going to take me there? When're you going to show me this place?"—and what's she do? Sits. Just sits, eyes not even moving, like she's stoned or drunk or just doing it to make him mad. To hell with her. Because if you're going to know anything about the town, you have to know Main Street. You have to know every bump, every crack, every tree and bush, every light pole, every shadow big enough to hide a cop car.

In the rear view mirror the Dari Delite, red-lettered specials in the window, recedes behind them. Like a memory. A dream almost, float-ing there, disconnected from anything but the hundreds of trips he's made up and down this street. And you have to know how that feels and why you do it. Kids drag the strip in Wichita, too, but it's not the same. There you can go anywhere—movies, drive-ins, parties—here the pattern is fixed: down Main to the end by the Downtowner, make a U-turn and head back up to the highway. Left and you go out for another turn-around at the Baitshop, maybe honking your horn under the underpass. Right and you end up at the cemetery road, where later on there will be some good quarter-mile drag races. If you

stop off en route, it's at the pool hall or bowling alley downtown—
maybe the laundromat—or at the Dari Delite back up at the end of
Main, sitting on the hood of your car drinking Cokes and hooting
and yelling at whoever happens by.

There's nothing else like it. If you're too young to drive, you don't
count for much anyway. But if you do drive, you'll be on the street.
You'll be there from seven till eleven—later on Saturdays—because
everybody else you know, or want to, will be there, too. Up and down,
up and down. And you'll see the same people over and over. You'll say
and hear the same things night after night—girls and cars and school
and where you can find a drink or some dope, depending on how
adventurous you are.

She needs to know all that, to understand it. And she needs to
know that he, Ronnie Blue, used to be king of the strip. Any night he
was out, he would end up at the head of the parade, a train of cars
behind him clear out of sight downtown. Everybody following the
leader. But you have to know what you're doing. You can't drive too
fast or the cars will string out and break the line. Too slow and you
have to ride your clutch to keep your car from bucking around like
you've never been behind the wheel before. It takes skill. And nobody
was better at it than him.

Not only just driving, either—because you always have to stop at
some point and talk—usually to the person in the lead car coming
from the other direction. To do it right, you have to know how to ease
next to each other, within touching distance, but never doing so, of
course. And you have to hang an arm and head out the window just
so, passengers smiling as the two of you converse, saying enough, but
not too much:

"How you doing?"

"All right, what's happening?"

"Nothing. Just riding around."

"Seen Louie?"

"A while back. Has his dad's car. Him and Bear."

"Probably at Herman's, shooting pool. Want a game?"

A quick look at the girlfriend. There's always a girlfriend. No lead driver can be without one.

"Not right now."

"Yeah, yeah." A knowing grin.

"Catch you later maybe."

"Yeah, later."

"See you."

"See you."

Then starting up again at exactly the moment everyone behind you is ready to peel off and go around.

It's timing. Timing and knowing the town and the people, how much they can take and when to back off. And if you don't know that, you'll never make it. Here, at least, in a place like Bartlett's Junction.

But Charlene's never lived in a small town. She was born in Seattle, then moved to Oklahoma City, then to Wichita. So when she looks at Bartlett's Junction—when she manages to raise her head long enough—all she probably sees is a bunch of squat, dusty buildings that every twenty years get new fronts. This time it was pastel aluminum with matching awnings that run the length of the stores. Lots of glass, sidewalk to ceiling, so you can see better what's inside. But none of that changes. Some of the displays haven't been rotated in so long they've gone all grey, lettering a faint, faint white, like on ashes. And the people don't change much, either. You can name most all of them. They just get a little shorter and more wrinkled.

Occasionally a business will change locations—the newspaper moving a block south into the old dry goods store, the bowling alley into the old movie theater, the American Legion into the old beauty parlor, and Yost's, the lawyer's, office into the old radio and TV store. But sometimes only the names change, like the supermarket from IGA to Thrift to Jack and Jill, and the hardware from Burns' to Ace. And, of course, a few never change at all—locations, names or people. The drug stores and the hotel. The bank. They occupy the four corners of the major intersection downtown—Main and First Streets. To the right, just behind the bank, are the post office and a small electronics plant. To the left, a block from the hotel is the funeral home. The rest of the business district stretches like blue Monday wash from Morton's Drug Store to the Downtowner beer joint on the west side of the street, and from Al's Rexall to Mid-American Auto Repair on the east. Beyond them are an independent feed store being run out of business by the Co-op and the old Santa Fe depot with a commemorative marker honoring Russian Mennonite settlers and Turkey Red wheat. Finally, the Santa Fe tracks. Then Deever Creek. Then open land.

And that's the way it's been since he can remember. Change and no change. A sort of slow movement, something you don't notice has stopped until it does, like breathing.

At the bottom of Main he starts into a wide, lazy U-turn.

"So this is it," he says, arm out like a tour director. "This here's the place that made me what I am today."

"Huh!" She peers at him with one eye squinted shut.

The car coasts to a halt parallel to the curb, across faded yellow lines that show angle parking. But it doesn't matter. The wind is all that's sharing the street with them.

He kills the motor. "All right, what the hell is it? Out with it."

She shakes her head and looks away.

"You better tell me, because in about two minutes I'm going to be mighty pissed."

Her face is haggard, puffy, like her mother's when she's been out too late. Like an old bitch in heat who's been making the rounds.

"Is it still that goddamn hat? That what's eating you?"

"You said I could have one if we got dressed up. You lied to me."

"I forgot everything'd be closed." He strokes her hair, soft and silky brown. Glimmering. "That ain't lying."

"Don't know what else you'd call it."

"Ronnie Blue don't lie," wrapping a strand of hair around his hand.

"Ouch!"

"Ronnie Blue don't lie."

"That hurts."

"Does he?"

"Ron-nie!"

She's sitting as tall in the seat as she can, head tilted back and toward him. Her mouth is open, eyes fixed on a spot near his right ear. It has to hurt. Ronnie Blue does not lie.

Get them down, boy.

She has to know he means business.

All the way.

Even if she is too damn stubborn to admit she's wrong, tell him she's sorry.

Grab your ankles—grab them.

"No!"

Ass in the air, boy. Get your ass in the air.

"Uh-huh!"

Teach you to steal from me, you lying little bastard.

Kissing the hollow at the base of her neck, blood beating against his lips.

No.

"You're hurting me."

No.

"Ronnie!"

On top of Miller's Hill, where the grass is tallest and the land swells to meet the sky all around, thrashing it out there in that dusty, straw-smelling place, nothing paying them any mind but grasshoppers and birds, an old coyote.

"Ahhhh!"

He releases her. She crouches against her door, rubbing her scalp.

"I-do-not-lie."

"All right. Jesus, all right."

He starts the car and turns east on First Street. A half block down is Cora Gaul's hat shop. He parks and pulls her out of the car to the window.

"Find one you want."

"Let's just forget it, okay. No big deal."

"Pick one out."

"No, I really don't—"

"I mean it. If I said you'd get a hat, you'll get a goddamn hat."

Hands to either side of her face, she slides the length of the window and back. Stepping away, she points to a straw hat with a wide, floppy brim and a single row of yellow and white flowers around the band.

"But, really, it's all right if we don't get one. It'll be a lot of money."

"To hell with money. You're sure that's the one you want?"

"I think so," bringing the reflection of her dress in line with the hat, him beside her in his grey pleated slacks, maroon suspenders striping the open-necked white shirt with rolled-up sleeves. "Don't you?"

"Perfect," he says.

"You mean it?"

"I mean it. Let's go."

Nine o'clock and he's sweating. He puts the top down on the car, sun coating his head and shoulders like warm honey.

"You need one, too," she says.

"A hat?"

"A felt one with a big satin band." She's smiling. At least trying to. Her eyes aren't yet.

He hates arguments. When things get out of hand. Nobody in control. It's like being on a strange road and having your footfeed stick and your steering go out all at the same time. It's just no damn good. So they'll get the hats and she'll be back with him for real, and they can start the day over again. Right from the top. And when he finally does tell her about scaring hell out of Josh Billings, she'll laugh like she used to, her teeth big and white, her lips wet. She'll laugh at all his stories, and people will look at her and think how pretty she is, eyes following the outline of her legs up her dress, Adam's apples bobbing as they swallow. And then they'll glance at him, a little twitch of a smile, and nod, as if to say: "You've done real good, Ronnie Blue. You've got yourself a car and money and a pretty woman. Yes, sir, you've done all right." Sir, they'll say, and she'll hear it and lean against him all warm and soft. He'll put an arm around her and hook a thumb through his suspender, smiling back at them with a cock of his head and a wink. Before long, word will spread that he's back in town, a shiny new Ronnie Blue, back to celebrate his birthday with them. And they'll all come out to wish him well and more of the same.

When he and Charlene leave, there'll be a little let-down, disappoint-
ment that they couldn't have stayed longer.

"Ronnie?"

"Yeah?"

"I've been thinking. I don't see how you're going to pay for hats and
have anything left over. And that's really all the money we've got, ain't
it? I won't get paid again till next week, so maybe we ought to—"

He covers her mouth. "Now you let me take care of things, all
right? This is my place. I know how to get along here. I know how to
get along just fine. Trust me?"

"But we have to eat, Ronnie."

"Trust me."

Mrs. Gaul lives on Cottonwood Street across from where the
grade school used to be. Tract houses line that side of the block now,
differing only in color. Red, green and yellow boxes on sodded, tree-
less lots, vulnerable in the summer heat.

He parks in front of one, a face he doesn't remember peering from
behind heavy drapes. He waves. The drapes close.

His hand on her hip for the benefit of the person he knows will
be watching again from the window, he leads Charlene toward Mrs.
Gaul's, a low, green-roofed bungalow, its front porch shrouded in
evergreen and spirea bushes.

"Come on," he says. "She won't bite."

He pushes the buzzer. The floor jars. The window in the door rat-
tles, a frosted pane with a pine tree and a stag highlighted in the middle. The lace curtain goes back.

Mrs. Gaul's face has fallen. Melted, rather, folds of flesh descend-
ing in smooth layers around eyes, nose and mouth. Her hair, still
somewhat dark, hangs in a page-boy cut. Her glasses are large with
black rims, eyes switching back and forth behind them.

"Who is it?"

"It's Ronnie Blue, Mrs. Gaul. Chester Blue's boy?"

The curtain drops back into place. A chain lock falls, a bolt lock clacks. The door sticks, wobbles open.

"Sorry. I didn't recognize you there. You've been gone so darn long and there's so darn much meanness anymore a body can't be too careful."

The screen door is still locked. Behind it, she looks like someone in an old, grainy photograph, the kind you see on people's walls even when they don't know for sure whose picture it is.

"Yes, sir, folks move away and they change—don't we all, though?—and then when they don't get back very often, why, it's hard to keep up. Kids especially. They change the most, I guess."

"Yeah, I imagine so," he says.

"Why, you, I remember you with that long hair hot-rodding around town." She squints past them toward the street. "Yes, sir, that's the very same car right there. Still hot-rodding, I suppose."

"No, ma'am, not much. I'm a little too busy for that these days. And, well, I guess you just sort of outgrow it, too."

"Hmm. Where are you now?"

"Wichita."

"That's what I thought. Back for the Fourth, I suppose."

"Yes, ma'am."

"Be seeing your folks?"

"In a while."

"I run into your mama every so often at the grocery store. Hardly ever see your dad, though."

"He's never been one for getting out much."

"No, I suspect not."

"And he keeps pretty busy up at the salvage lot."

"I suppose there's a lot to do there."

"Yes, ma'am, there sure is."

"So—" She's looking at Charlene, who's standing to one side, pigeon-toed, hands clasped in front of her like some jerky high school kid about to be scolded for smoking in the bathroom.

He reaches out and pulls her to him. "Now I'll tell you why we stopped by, Mrs. Gaul. We just got into town, see, Charlene and me, and since she's never been here I took her to see the sights. Well, we just happened to be going by your shop and she tells me to stop and she jumps out and runs over to the window. It was that straw hat—that big one with all the flowers around the top. Right in front there. Well, she says, 'Ronnie, I want that hat,' and I told her there wasn't any way we could get a hat on the Fourth. But she told me she wanted it real bad and wasn't going to be happy till she had it. So I said we'd try. I said we'd stop by and see if there was any chance at all of getting it. And, well, here we are."

"That hat costs thirty-five dollars," Mrs. Gaul says.

"Price ain't no problem."

"Oh? And just what is it you're doing there in Wichita?"

"Mechanics," he says. "Cars and trucks. You know."

She glances at his hands, nails and knuckles without a trace of grease.

"Matter of fact," he says, "I just got promoted about a month ago. Shop foreman. I'd a lot rather be in there doing the actual fixing of the motors, but—" He shrugs.

"I don't know. I really don't." Mrs. Gaul glances around, as if looking for someone to consult. "I just hate to have to go down and open up on a holiday."

"Sure. I understand. Just thought we'd take a chance."

"But—Well, shoot, seeing as how you're from out of town now and all, well—Why not? Won't take more than a minute, and we just shouldn't forget who our friends are, now should we? No, sir. So you kids go on down and I'll meet you there soon as I get my shoes on."

"We sure appreciate this, Mrs. Gaul. We really do."

Back in the car, he salutes the person in the window and squeezes Charlene's knee.

"See there? Nothing to it."

"Why'd you tell her all that stuff?"

"My god, woman, you think she was going to open up for just any-body?" He turns the corner, the thrum of tires on brick pavement. "Look in the glove compartment. Should be an old checkbook in there."

"You can't do that."

"You want the hat or not?"

"Sure, but—"

"Sometimes I can't figure you out. First you do, then you don't. I don't know. I mean, what's the bitch now? You worried we're going to break that old woman up? That it? Well, let me tell you something: she's so rich already she's not going to know the difference. You don't think she had all those locks on that door just to protect her old body, do you? Besides, it ain't like stealing anyway. We'll get her the money as soon as you get paid next week. I'll give her a call and straighten it all out. If that don't suit you, say so now."

They're standing at the window when Mrs. Gaul drives up, the smell of burnt paint from the motor of her new Chevrolet blowing past them.

"Nice car," he says.

"Comfortable anyway." She pushes open the door of the shop. A bell jingles inside.

Despite the tang of dyes from hats and a few bolts of material, the shop smells musty. Crumbling mortar and bricks. Wet plaster. Old floorboards under the carpet you could never get clean. The place used to be a barbershop, and it makes him itch to think of all the hair that must still be floating around.

Mrs. Gaul clumps to the window and lifts the hat from the stand. Gingerly, as if afraid it might fall apart.

Close up, it looks like it could, too. The flowers aren't hooked on very well, the inside seams are rough, and in one place on top the weave is broken. He smiles, wondering who's trying to get who here. But it does look good when Charlene puts it on, he has to admit that. Kind of like a broad frame around her face. And she was right about it finishing off the outfit. It does, real well.

"We'll take it," he says. "And while you're at it, you wouldn't happen to have any men's hats, would you?"

She lowers her head, hand to her face. "I stopped carrying them a few years ago. Just didn't seem to move very well. But, you know, now that I think about it, I might just have a couple I couldn't return left here in the back."

She comes out with a stack of boxes. Charlene wrinkles her nose at the first one—a bowler-type that looks like you'd need an umbrella to go with it—but when she sees the second, she jumps and claps her hands. "Put it on! Put it on!"

It's old and grey, just like she said she wanted, with a wide brim tipped down at the front, a sharp crease in the crown. All he needs is a moustache and he could be a gangster in one of those '30s cops and robbers movies.

"I can give you a good price on that one," Mrs. Gaul says.

"No, now I don't want you cheating yourself."

"We'll figure something," she says, jotting numbers on a pad.

"You don't mind a check, do you?"

Her pen stops.

"We really didn't plan on this, you see, and I want to be sure we still have enough cash left for a good time. You understand."

She's writing again. "Sure, that'll be fine. Just make it out to Gaul's Hat Shop."

He fills in the check and hands it to her. She waves it in front of her face like a little fan.

"You know," she says, "it's funny how things get connected in your brain. Maybe it's this check or that hat of yours or goodness knows what, but I can't for the life of me get John Klein off my mind. You and him was in the same class, wasn't you?"

"That's right. I'd say we were pretty good friends, as a matter of fact."

"I thought so. I thought I remembered him in that car of yours."

"Yes, ma'am, me and him had some good times all right."

"I don't suppose that's what everybody'd call it," her face lifting in a smile. "But then from the looks of things I'd say you both turned out all right. He's back now, you know."

"In Bartlett's Junction?"

"Working at the bank with his dad. He's such a nice boy. We're sure glad to have him."

"Golly, I haven't seen him in so long. How is he, anyway?"

"All right, as far as I know. Getting kind of sweet on one of the new teachers, from what I hear. But we need more of that, too. More good young people coming back and staying. Raising families."

"John Klein, huh? Son of a gun."

"Now you boys sang together, too, didn't you?"

"Yes, ma'am, we did a lot of singing. Why?"

"I don't know. Just wondering if that was the reason I thought of him right now. It's so funny how those things pop into your head."

"It is," Ronnie Blue nods. "It really is."

"Maybe you boys can get together or something while you're here," she says. "Wouldn't that be nice if you could?"

"Very nice. But if we're going to get around to it, we'd best be moving on now. People to see, things to do, you know."

She smiles like a mother who has just arranged for her children's happiness.

"And we want to thank you again for the trouble, Mrs. Gaul. These hats are going to make our day." He stops at the door. "Oh, and listen, if you happen to run into John, tell him I'm here, all right? All right, we'll see you later."

Getting into the car, they both adjust their hats before driving off, Mrs. Gaul at the window waving goodbye.

He turns north on Main, toward the highway and the junkyard. Charlene laughs, moving over against him. He puts his arm around her, hand sliding to her breast. A lone pickup approaches. He lifts his finger from the steering wheel. The driver, high in his cab, grins with one side of his mouth and cocks his thumb, English-style.

Scooting down in his seat, he takes a firmer hold on Charlene. "There now, didn't I tell you? Didn't I tell you things'd start jumping as soon as Ronnie Blue hit town? They remember me here. They love me, they can't help it. And you're just lucky as hell to be along."

4

Linda is waiting for him on Mrs. Mayhew's front porch, curled around a book in the swing, Bert the cat napping beside her. His tail and her foot twitch harmoniously. She glances up, smiling and waving, then finishes the sentence she was reading before closing the book on a marker. Rising slowly, gathering her things, she has the look about her of a woman who knows who she is and what she wants. And at this point, that seems to include him, John Klein.

The first time he saw her was at a high school basketball game shortly after she'd moved to town. She'd just come through the door of the gym and was scanning the bleachers for a place to sit—more likely for a familiar face, since there were dozens of empty seats. And he remembers thinking how pretty she seemed. Full face, dark eyes, lovely brown hair swept back over her ears. A good figure, too, slender and well-proportioned. There's no doubt that she would have turned his head anywhere, but then he would have gone on about his business. He wouldn't have just kept staring, as he did that night, far past the point of impoliteness. He knew he was being rude, but he didn't care. He simply couldn't take his eyes off her. Even when she looked at him, shaking her head as if to say he really shouldn't be making such a fuss. He smiled oh but yes he should and was about to go down and tell her so right then and there when she spotted Russ Barnes, the grade school principal, himself a bachelor, and went to sit with him.

The second time he saw her was in his office at the bank. She'd come to check on an overdraft on her account. She was embarrassed, but hardly submissive, saying things like she'd never had a decent experience with a bank and every banker she'd known was arrogant and condescending. He asked where she was from. "Missouruh," the *uh* worn like a club membership on her tongue. He nodded and said he wasn't surprised she'd had problems, then, since it was his under-standing that people over there could be pretty stubborn. She laughed, a wonderful sparkle coming to her eye he still wishes he had a picture of. Then he called Ron Padgett and told him there'd been a mistake on Linda Grey's returned check, he should send it on through again. She thanked him, blushing now because of what she'd said about banks and bankers. He told her it was their earnest desire to make her experience with them as pleasant as possible, and asked if she wouldn't like to go over to Trudy's for a cup of coffee.

She grew up in Maryville, Missouri. Her father teaches music at Northwest Missouri State. Her mother is an accountant at a local medical clinic. In their eyes, she ran away from home when she decided to go to college at the University of Missouri-Kansas City instead of going to Northwest Missouri State and living at home as her sisters had. Living at home, marrying at home, never leaving home.

But Bartlett's Junction? he asked. Why had she come here?

She looked at him, deadpan, and said two places had offered her a job and he should have seen the other one.

Yeah, he could imagine.

And what about him? she wanted to know. Had he come back for some reason other than having a congenital predisposition toward banking?

So she had noticed him. She had been asking about him. What was she expecting him to say?

There were probably lots of reasons, he told her. Home. Family. Not so much friends, though. Most of them had gone away and not come back. But a few like him had, and more were doing it all the time. And that was good. That was great. That was really exciting. He had some ideas he wanted to try out. Some dreams, you might say. But he needed help to see them through. They all had to do with the town and how to make it a better place to live. But that wasn't going to be easy, not when you considered that the place still existed after more than a century, not because of good planning or the town's inherent charm, but by virtue of sheer stubbornness. Why, it had even weathered his great-grandfather, Theophilus Klein, who was largely responsible for the town's not having the refinery that went to Potwin, the Santa Fe roundhouse that went to Newton, the dairy that went to Hillsboro. She had to understand that Bartlett's Junction had missed enough chances for growth to kill less reactionary communities. But somehow it was still here. Somehow it had survived. And now was the time, he thought, to revive it, to bring new life to it, new hope, a sense of the future. Which was a big reason why he'd come back and why he planned to stay.

She said how noble it all sounded, and he blushed then and went on to admit as how another big draw—maybe even the biggest, just as it had been with her—was his job. He had a nice office, nice people to work with, a nice salary. And he figured he probably had a pretty good chance for advancement.

She laughed then finally, throwing her head back, and he remembers acutely wanting to kiss her.

He asked if she'd go to the next basketball game with him. Then there was dinner in Wichita, a play, a concert, a long weekend in Kansas City, eating at Bryant's and watching the Royals start their season. They flew to Denver for a music festival. They did and do what they please when they please. And whatever or wherever it is, it's done intensely. They work hard and play hard and have become inseparable. Objections that might have been raised about the dubious legality of parts of their relationship have simply never surfaced. Or if they have, they've been spoken quietly, in the privacy of the home. For Linda Grey and John Klein have become symbols of the new Bartlett's Junction. They are the darlings of the town, beautiful people, vicarious lives. And besides, everyone knows that in the end real love always leads to marriage. And a family. Mowed lawns and trimmed hedges. Homemade vanilla ice cream on Sunday afternoons, children playing on lawns all across town.

Not an unpleasant notion, for he does love her. Senselessly, mindlessly, beyond all reason. He wants her—this crazy, happy, cunning, unpredictable woman skipping along the walk toward him, breasts dancing under a bright yellow shell, a mischievous grin on her face. He wants her as his lover, his wife, the mother of his children, his support, his critic, his friend—all those silly things he used to laugh at other people for thinking. He needs her.

A familiar rush, a cold streak right through the middle of his insides. Fear. Fear that someday he'll wake up and find she's been a dream, or that someday she'll decide to leave—him, the town, all the things they've planned on. Fear that, for god knows whatever reason, things just won't work out and he'll be alone again.

He can't stand that. He can't stand thinking about life without her, or of her life with someone else, his life with someone else, what they would talk about, what they would do, how they would do it. Who?

She opens the door and slides across the seat. "Umm," her hand on the back of his head. "Umm, again," biting his lip. "You taste good. Must have just brushed your teeth. Umm." She sits up, smoothing her top. "So where've you been? I was about ready to send out the highway patrol."

"I'm only late, not missing. Are you mad?"

"No. I just like to be with you."

"Let's go somewhere and be together then."

"But this is important to your folks," she says. "They've been looking forward to it so much."

"I haven't."

"You've mentioned that before," she says.

"They won't do anything but argue about that damn portrait, and you know it."

"Maybe not. Maybe this time—"

"Why don't we go up to the lake for a while? Have some peace and quiet."

"We promised, John. Besides, it's not going to be forever. I told your mother we couldn't stay late."

"So when's she leaving?" he says, glancing at Mrs. Mayhew's house.

"Mrs. Calhoun's picking her up for services at a quarter to eleven. The coast should be clear from then on."

They've never made love in Linda's room. Linda's blue room. Pristine blue. The room Mary Mayhew fixed up for the daughter she never had. Eternally virginal.

"I'm ready now," he says.

"So am I. But she isn't."

"Praying?"

She nods. "Since seven. She won't stop till ten-thirty, either.

Enough time to get dressed. It's been like this every morning for a week now. Just like a Moslem."

"She'd die if she heard you say that." Mary Mayhew adores Linda. In her eyes, she can do no wrong. Which is good for Linda, good for him.

"But it's the truth," she says. "Isn't it? You've seen her."

He has, Mary Mayhew in her living room, kneeling on a sofa cushion, voice lifted to Almighty God for protection from Communists, hippies, Jews, coloreds, dope fiends, fornicators and any other Godless force bent on destroying her and what she holds dear. She and her friends gathered spiritually together, like cattle bunching at the onset of a storm.

"We really shouldn't make fun of her," he says, putting the car in gear. "She's so afraid of everything."

"Only if it's different."

"Such a sweetheart," he says.

"Me? What about you? I heard what you used to say before she gave all that money for the tennis courts. She was an obstructionist, for one. And an old biddy."

"Yeah, but—"

"She was praying for *them* this morning, too. Something about building sound bodies and spirits."

"Bless her old soul," he says.

"Bless her pocketbook and powers of persuasion, you mean."

They pass along the front edge of the park to the main gates and through them onto the half mile dirt track that years ago sported fashionable Sunday afternoon sulky races. It's even rumored that the legendary Dan Patch once ran here and won. But now, with the exception of final preparations for the carnival near the wall at the north end of the football field, the park is dusky and quiet, dark blotches of shade patching the ground under enormous old elm trees. A quarter of the way around the track in a clearing down from a cluster of picnic tables near the swimming pool are the new courts, temporary metal bleachers along one side glimmering in the sunlight.

Linda's right. Without Mary Mayhew there might not be new tennis courts. When he started the drive to build them, the going was so slow he thought he would have to resort to a bond issue, no simple matter considering that not a single one has passed in Bartlett's Junction in over fifteen years. What he had forgotten, of course, was Mary Mayhew and her crowd. Linda suggested that he present her with the idea, and it was she who softened the old woman up with talk of goodness and wholesomeness. In a month he had more money than he needed. The courts are to be opened officially at one o'clock today, with an exhibition match between two ranked area players.

On around the back side of the park. More trees, more here than anywhere in town. Great open spaces under them that later in the day will be so crowded it'll be hard to find a place to spread a picnic blanket.

"It looks so nice," she says. "Isn't it amazing what a little extra paint and trimming can do? Makes you want to sit right down and relax, like you're in your own back yard. And that's just how you wanted people to feel. You should be proud."

He is. But he's also tired. The paint and trimming alone took two weeks of negotiations with the city council. But it does look good, and he's glad. He's always glad once things are finished. And people will notice, after the carnival gets going and they start out and about, more and more coming toward evening for the largest fireworks display in Kansas.

The fireworks started in 1876. Modestly, getting bigger and better, until they became the grandest in the state—the town's one great claim to fame. And this year they may be the best ever. Will be, since he's chairman of the fireworks committee. Another of Linda's suggestions. When the opening came up and his name was submitted, she said: "You've been looking for things that need doing, so do it." He did, and he did it well. So well that all those folks from Wichita and Hutchinson and Salina won't be able to stop talking about what they've seen. They'll go back home and tell their friends and neighbors, tell them in such glowing terms that they'll want to come the next year, too. Come early and spend the day and all the money they brought. The less they go home with, the more fun they'll figure they've had. A fundamental principle. And the more money they spend, the more the town will be able to afford things for them to spend it on. And everybody will get happier and happier, while he gets tireder and tireder.

"We could always go to Wichita and catch a flight to Acapulco."

"Just one more day," she says.

"But I've had it. I've done enough good for a while."

"You can't let up now. Not with the momentum you've got going."

"Aren't you tired?" he says.

"Not really."

"Don't you ever wish you could just chuck it and let somebody else be responsible?"

"I suppose so," she says.

"Well—"

"You'll be okay," her hand coming up his leg. "Once breakfast is over and we're concentrating on something else."

"Dessert?"

She smiles.

At the three-quarter mark—he used to run the track in cross country meets before they started using the golf course—a stone wall sections off the WPA football field and baseball diamond. Elaborate wooden lattices which will give form to the larger fireworks displays rise in the morning light like the skeletal remains of creatures that might have once grazed in this very spot.

"Where's George?" she says.

"Been here and gone from the looks of it. He was probably out at five to beat the heat and went back home now for a nap."

They leave the park as they came, through the main gate, and drive east toward downtown. A block away, just beyond the Rock Island tracks lined with boxcars, they pass under the skein of augers that relay wheat back and forth between the Co-op elevator and the steel Butler building. Their tires pick up the patter of brick pavement.

In the middle of the intersection of Main and First Streets a hand-lettered sign cemented in a barrel announces baseball and softball games, the tennis match, a charitable concession at the park.

There isn't much activity yet. The town looks pallid, bleak, dust devils playing in shadows of buildings, flags waving to empty streets.

Near Mrs. Gaul's store, he slows, nearly stops. Ronnie Blue's Chevy is parked in front of the door, Mrs. Gaul's car pulled up directly behind. He can see movement inside, but can't distinguish one person from another.

"A little holiday profit," Linda says.

"Looks like it."

"If there's any to be made, she'll know about it."

"You're right about that," he says.

But this time she's met her match. If he knows Ronnie Blue, Mrs. Gaul hasn't seen a penny of cash, and won't. He can almost hear the cock and bull story he gave to get her to open up. The guy's a natural. And he'll lay odds it was funny, too. He's been with him lots of times when things started out funny, but somewhere in the middle they turned sour, and he always got embarrassed but went along with it anyway because Ronnie Blue was doing it. Like what's probably going on in there now.

That kind of stuff appealed to him once, setting people up and knocking them over their own foibles. Back then it seemed justified, being smarter than everybody else, teaching them lessons in spite of themselves. But he doesn't feel that way anymore, no matter how tired he is, no matter how out of sorts. It's like trying on old clothes and finding out they don't fit the way you remembered. And maybe Ronnie Blue's different, too, and he's just not giving him the benefit of the doubt. But five years ago when they parted, the guy had no plans, nothing to grow on. And here he is, looking the same, driving the same car. The truth is, he probably hasn't changed a bit, but he'll think he has, and when they finally do meet today—Bartlett's Junction is too small for that not to happen—he'll tell all about ripping Mrs. Gaul off and expect a good laugh, like in the old days. And when he doesn't get it, what then?

"John?"

"Humh?"

"What's wrong?"

"Nothing."

"Yes, there is."

"No, really. It's nothing."

She glances back at the shop. Is she wondering old lover, old friend, old hat?

"Just somebody I know. Somebody I used to know."

"Who?"

"It doesn't make any difference now," he says, putting his arm around her. "So don't worry about it. I'm not."

They turn south on Cottonwood, Ronnie Blue's Chevy a glancing speck in the rear view mirror.

"Any bets on what Mom'll have cooked up for us?" he says, zigzag-ging over the Santa Fe tracks to keep from hitting bottom.

"How do you mean 'cooked up'?"

"Food-wise."

As they pass the Co-op feed mill and filling station and cross the Deever Creek bridge out of town, they talk about how his mother will have been up since five-thirty making biscuits and sweet rolls, fruit salad, sausage, eggs, hash browns, fresh sliced tomatoes, juice, coffee and tea. Finished now, the kitchen back to its original, immaculate condition, she'll be standing at the counter, wiping her hands on her apron, maybe allowing herself a few sips of coffee as she stares out the window over the sink, waiting. With a full view of the town and every major approach to the house, she'll see the car as soon as it tops the hill up from Bly's Corner and she'll hang her apron in the pantry, straighten her dress and call to the living room: "Bud? Put away the paper now. The children are here."

He and Linda both dislike the house. Huge, white, trimmed with all manner of Victorian frill, a railed porch spreading ironically across its face, it squats on the only sizable hill around like a fat potentate, as out of place in this landscape as was the man who built it.

Wiley Bartlett arrived at what was then called Oxbow Station in the summer of 1872. The story goes that he was the only passenger who got off the train that day, and he stood for what must have been a long while, staring at the depot, the combination general store-hotel-saloon and three frame houses propped on the prairie like a child's play town, as if he might have gotten off at the wrong stop and wasn't quite sure what he should do now. Then, with great care, he dusted himself off, adjusted his velvet coat and ruffled cuffs and walked into the town, already considering how to remake it in his own image.

The only account of those early days comes from Theophilus Klein, John Klein's great-grandfather and Wiley Bartlett's friend, partner and eventual worst enemy. It is a history John Klein learned from the time he was a small child—much as monarchs are indoctrinated in royal genealogy, he always thought.

The elder Klein came to Kansas the spring of 1873. He was everything Wiley Bartlett was not—staid, cautious, conservative. They were immediately attracted to each other and formed a relationship that flourished for nearly eighteen years. In fact, it was one day short of their eighteenth anniversary that Wiley Bartlett stole fifty thousand dollars from the bank he and Theophilus Klein owned and made off for points west.

An act of such treachery and meanness was unimaginable, and Theophilus Klein closed himself up in his study for a week to think things through.

Wiley Bartlett had always been dissatisfied, yes, but that was in large part what also made him such a perfect partner. Continually at odds with the status quo, Bartlett became the visionary force behind the community. It was he who conceived of the sawmill to supply building materials for the town, the grinding mill to supply flour, the smithy to produce the great sod-busting plows necessary to farm the land. It was he who suggested that they start a bank. It was he who laid out plans for what was then the most magnificent park in the state. But the accomplishment he was most proud of himself, and the one for which the people renamed the town in his honor, was when he succeeded in getting the Rock Island Railroad to build a line to intersect the Santa Fe at the southwest edge of town, thus making

Bartlett's Junction the only place in the state, outside of Kansas City, with two major railroads at its disposal.

But there was also the other side of Wiley Bartlett, Theophilus Klein was to say. The irresponsible, anti-social, debauching Wiley Bartlett, who in the beginning would take holidays to Kansas City or St. Louis to indulge the darker side of himself, then return, purged, ready to get back to work. Later, as he became less enthused with his visionary role, he more openly indulged his appetites, in flagrant violation of all laws and rules of civilized behavior. In 1886, he built his house—his magnum opus, he called it, his final will and testament—and peopled it with whores and gamblers and known crooks. The townspeople tolerated him. Some still even loved him. He was, after all, *the* Wiley Bartlett, without whom there might not be a Bartlett's Junction. And the more he tested, the more they indulged him, for as long as he kept his perversions to his house, they were not directly affected. Taking their money from the bank, however, was an entirely different matter.

Theophilus Klein, emerging from his week-long isolation, announced to the town what had happened, but that there was no reason for panic. He would stand the loss from his own resources and see to it that everyone's accounts were covered in full—letting it be known that such an offer was not made without considerable financial strain.

So the crisis was weathered, with the effect that the town came to see Theophilus Klein as its new leader, its new moral force. It was a responsibility he accepted reluctantly, for he knew he was not strong enough to avoid opposing anything Wiley Bartlett might have supported. And the town came to a dead stop, where it has rested for eighty-eight years.

In 1911, twenty years after Bartlett's infamous deed, Theophilus

Klein felt justice had finally been done when he learned that Wiley Bartlett had died broke and dissipated in a San Francisco brothel. Ten years after that, still alive and more successful than ever, the old man allowed himself a slight smile.

What remains of Wiley Bartlett can be seen in the tracks of a now bankrupt railroad, the park and the fireworks display, the first of which he personally financed to help celebrate the nation's centennial. And there is also his house, of course, and the town's name, for no one could think of anything very clever or kind to do with Klein.

Bartlett's house was bought shortly after he left by a rancher who added a barn and several outbuildings to the hilltop and allowed goats, sheep and a donkey to graze the two acre lawn. Bartlett would have sneered at the sight, but the rancher, a practical and realistic man, never gave a second thought to putting that much open land to use. Within a year, all of Wiley Bartlett's careful landscaping had been eaten, discharged and trodden back into the earth.

The house stayed in the rancher's family until 1975, when his son decided to retire to Colorado. His son in turn did not want the house because of its unmanageable size, and, as it was on the market for a good price and was of particular historical interest to him, Bud Klein bought the place, had it refurbished and moved in.

John Klein has always considered the move an act of revenge, a final twist of the knife in the spirit of Wiley Bartlett. His parents would never admit as much, of course, saying instead that they needed the extra space for entertaining and—with a wink—for all the grandchildren they expect to have around. But it's not home to him, and never will be, remote on its hill, inaccessible to anyone not invited. The house is so intimidating, so grand, it gives the impression that those who live there have chosen to separate themselves from all but a select few. In that way, he has trouble seeing the difference between his parents and Wiley Bartlett. As Linda says: "Sometimes it's hard to tell who's getting revenge on whom."

The house has been nicely redone, there's no denying that. New trees and shrubs and a lush mat of Bermuda grass have freshened the place, lessened the effect of its mass. And once inside, you feel warm, homey, surrounded by early American furniture, Williamsburg hues, natural woodwork and floors, copper and brass. The enveloping arms and relieved smiles. You have come. You have not failed them after all. Your own smiles, which they take as love, but which are brought on during the slow procession through the house—comments on small changes here and there and how good they look—because no matter what the furnishings, it is impossible ever to forget who designed the place and for what. Window recesses in the living and dining rooms, for instance. Deep recesses. Deeper than necessary to protect the house from cold drafts. Deep enough to accommodate a settee or day bed, comfortably out of sight behind drawn drapes. Or the curious revolving bookcases in the library, with just enough space for a person to stand behind them. Or the several accesses to each bedroom, which when opened up, give a serial view of all five chambers.

"Such a waste," his mother says. "Such silliness. I don't know what I'm ever going to do about some of it. Do you? Not without rebuilding the whole place. So I guess we'll just have to learn to live with it, won't we?"

"And that old thing," leading them off to breakfast, he and Linda hand in hand past the portrait of Wiley Bartlett hanging over the mantel. "You'll have to ask your father when that's coming down."

A smirking, self-satisfied face peers back, distant as a reflection in an old mirror.

5

$\mathcal{A}$rdell Blue stares at them through the rusty wire of the screen door. Eyes wide, like they've been painted on, ping pong ball eyes saying nothing, the rest of her face long and hollow, misty in the faint light, thin little mouth open, tongue lying like a slug against her lower lip.

"Mama? You all right, Mama?"

The tongue retreats, lips screwing up.

"It's me, Ronnie."

"I know it's you, what do you take me for? It's just—"

"Should've called ahead, huh?"

"You know that ain't necessary. I'm just surprised. Didn't expect you is all," eyes shifting to his left.

"This here's Charlene. My girl. I brought her to see the sights—and to meet you and Daddy."

"What's that?" his old man's voice growling out of the darkness. A bear hunter. He always imagined his old man as a bear hunter, able to growl down any grizzly. "Who's there?"

"Get your shirt on and come up here and see," his mother says. "We've got some company."

A cough, deep and wet. A thud, the thump of stockinged feet on carpet, Chester Blue's face fuzzing into view behind his wife's.

"I'll be a son of a bitch. What're you doing here, boy?"

"Just came to see you."

"Last time you was here it cost me five hundred dollars."

"This is Charlene. I've been telling her all about you."

"Well, little lady, you'd be one hell of a lot better off finding yourself somebody else to play around with. This boy's nothing but trouble. A real mess."

"Now, Chester, you leave Ronnie be. He's come visiting, and that's all. No more bad-mouthing."

"Ain't nothing but the truth and you know it."

She steps between her husband and son and pushes open the screen door. "No sense talking like strangers, now is there? Come on in. Have you had breakfast?"

"Hell no, he ain't. Why should he when he knows he can get a free one here?"

"I'll see what I can find. Make yourselves at home now. Charlene—that's right, ain't it—maybe you can get you and Ronnie some coffee, if you drink it. We always do, always have a pot on. Now, let's see," hand to her mouth, as if trying to remember what she was about to do. She darts toward the kitchen, Charlene following almost meekly, head turning side to side as she goes.

Junk has crept up to the house, onto the porch. Like dust. Like an uncontrollable mold that threatens soon to cover everything and everybody, leaving them bleached as another freezer, empty-eyed as another gutted engine block. And the smell—dirty grease, dried mud, vapors oozing from the hot earth on a summer day, spiky weeds, corroded batteries, stale, rusty water, insides of old iceboxes, rotting upholstery, oil-soaked boards, sweat from a thousand hours under the sun, soap and deodorant glossing over the grime.

It is a deformed place, warty with heaps of rubbish, carcasses of cars, appliances, boilers, oil tanks, glass that won't really break, piles of pistons, generators, transmissions, wheels, axles, radiators and tires yet to be sorted through, most of them from vehicles so old no one drives them anymore, grown over in a tangle of bind weed, itch weed, grass higher than a man's head, where anything from wasps to snakes to mad dogs can lie in wait. Stuff that's not even useful in a junkyard. It should be cleaned up, scrapped out, put in order, moved back to a respectable distance. Every time he comes here, he leaves feeling dirty, diseased, and goes home to soak in the tub and scrape at his skin until it's raw, until it hurts so much he can't stand it anymore. But it's still there even then. Always. In his brain.

"So, boy," his old man says. "What is it you want this time?"

"I just come visiting is all."

Straw hat on his shaved head, skin chestnut brown and shiny, eyes hard as marble, his old man squints at him, just squints from that square face, like he's going blind or something.

"Nothing else. Just visiting," Ronnie Blue says again, the arm of the sofa scratchy under his palm.

"No money, now. There ain't going to be no goddamn money."

"I don't want any. I don't need any. All right?"

"Don't sass me, boy," the anchor tattooed on his old man's biceps rippling as he pulls himself erect in the chair. "I just want that to be clear, you hear? Just want it to be clear."

"It's clear."

"Before you get to talking. You and your goddamn poppycock ideas, why, you get started and you can talk anybody out of or into anything. That how you got in that girl's pants, boy? Talk your way in? I figure that's about the only way you could manage. But words is cheap. Words is real cheap, and once people find out that's all you are, what you say then ain't worth a damn, not a good goddamn."

There's a faint hum in the air he can't place, like a transformer, only less mechanical. It's broken off and on by the sound of a truck or car on the highway, then returns softly to his hearing.

Charlene brings them coffee, touching his hand lightly and smiling, as if to tell him it's okay, she's on his side.

When she leaves, he stares at the rectangle of sunlight drawn by the open window, his father's voice a backdrop to the glare.

"Like that bakery business, boy. A bakery, for Christ's sake, where they bake bread. Owned by some guy you said you knew, right? But you didn't, did you? Some flophouse Johnny who fed you a line. Worked in a doughnut shop, most likely, to get booze money. Hell of an investment, boy, a hell of an investment. Make us both rich, you said. Now just how much booze you think you can buy for five hundred dollars?"

Blurred shadows float in the light, faded grass and trees beyond. Again and again, one after another in the same pattern. He smiles.

"That's right, boy," his old man goes on, taking the smile for agreement. "Probably enough to kill him, don't you think?"

Bees. He leans toward the window. The hum is louder. A hive between the walls. Bees swarming all over—a honeycomb, his old man's face, mad when they discover the fraud and stinging. Stinging. He grins.

"Ain't that goddamn funny. It's my money, remember, money I ain't never going to see again."

"I told you I'd pay you back."

"Sure, and I hear it's supposed to snow tomorrow, too."

"You want it now?" Ronnie Blue pulls out the sixty dollars he has folded in his pocket so that it looks like a couple of hundred.

"Where would you get that kind of money, boy? Steal it?"

Less annoying than gnats, the bees drop away, stingers hanging spent from torn abdomens. He remembers once flying at his old man in a rage, arms windmilling, fists bruising against the body he later thought must be made of stone instead of flesh, his old man finally holding him at bay with a hand to his forehead, laughing as he sank to his knees in tears.

But he's done with that now. No more crying. Not for his old man, not for Carl, not for a damn dog. He's Ronnie Blue, and Ronnie Blue don't cry.

His mother swims before him, blinks into focus.

"It ain't much. Eggs and bacon and grits. Coffee. But it's filling. So come on and eat. Chester, you coming, too, or are you finished?"

"No, I'll be along. This is a family gathering, ain't it? A re-union? So it wouldn't do to have me out here all by myself, would it?"

Ronnie Blue and Charlene sit across from each other at the kitchen table, feet touching under it. His old man turns a chair around backwards and hooks his arms over the top, fingers intertwined like he's about to pray. But he just smiles. A squinty-eyed smile to keep you from knowing what he's thinking or where he's looking. Except Ronnie Blue can tell. He's giving Charlene one of those goings-over that makes you feel like you've been standing naked too long in a hot wind. And when it finally hits her what's happening, her cheeks flush and her foot shoots halfway up his leg. He closes his knees over it, her toes wiggling, burrowing.

He eats far beyond his hunger, sending his mother to the stove again and again. She laughs, tentatively at first, as if it's something she's not used to, then openly, shaking her head and saying, "I sure don't know where you're putting it. To look at you, a body'd think you didn't eat at all."

"It's the good cooking," Charlene says. "That and being home. You're always hungrier when you're at home."

"Well, I'm just glad you kids come by, that's all. Makes this a real special day. Don't it, Chester? Seems like we just never get together much anymore. Too busy, I guess. But it's still a shame, you not getting back home more often, Ronnie, since folks is always asking about you. Where you're living now, what you're doing. Whether you're married yet. They're always wanting to know that, saying how nice looking you are and all. And I tell them you said you wasn't going to be an easy catch and it'd take somebody pretty quick on their feet to get you." She refills their coffee cups. "Now, I'm not saying Charlene ain't. Not for a minute, so don't take me wrong."

"Oh, I'll bet she's fast enough, all right," his old man says. "I'll bet she's got just whatever it takes. That right, boy?"

"That's right."

"Well, now, is there something you're wanting to tell us?" his mother says, sideways to the stove, spatula raised expectantly.

"What the hell's got into you, woman? You know damn good and well that ain't the way things is done these days." He thrusts himself at Charlene and Ronnie, head and shoulders like a battering ram. "Is it, now?"

Charlene smiles. Ronnie Blue stares at his plate and says, "As a matter of fact, we have talked about getting married. But we're not ready yet. We want to wait a while, get ourselves together first. You know."

"Think it through careful-like, you mean?" his old man says. "Same way you go about everything?"

"I really don't see how you'd know, since you never listen."

His old man's arms flex against the chair back, lifting him halfway out of the seat.

"What can I get you?" his mother says. "Eggs? Grits? There's one more piece of bacon here."

Charlene taps his leg with her foot. He looks away from his old man. The chair squeaks again under Chester Blue's weight.

"Nothing else for me, Mama," he says, wiping up egg yolk with a crust of toast.

She sits finally at the end of the table opposite her husband. Looking at the two of them, he wonders why they stay together. Maybe it's just habit. Maybe they've been married so long they wouldn't know what to do if they weren't. He's seen pictures of his mother as a young woman: good looking, slender, gussied up and posed. Dressed the same, Charlene could pass for her sister. There aren't any pictures of his father, except one Navy shot. In it he looks the same as now, maybe a little less weathered. And handsome. The man is handsome. He can see why his mother might have been attracted to him. Once, until she found out what a son of a bitch he is. But maybe that was all it took. Maybe he, Ronnie Blue, is the result and they ended up stuck with each other, like it or not. If so, neither of them has talked about it—around him at least. The only thing he's ever heard, in fact, is his old man's denial that he has a child at all. It should be clear to anybody with eyes, he says: why, he don't look like a Blue, talk like a Blue or act like a Blue. For sure, no Blue would ever sing, prancing around up in front of people, sissy shit like that. And Blues are a close lot. They stay together, help each other out when need be. They never forget who they are or where they come from. They're family, by god, which, according to his old man, he has never learned the value of.

"So catch us up," his mother says, fidgeting with the napkin holder, the salt and pepper shakers. "What are you doing now? Still working for that nice man—what's his name—Carl?"

He leans back, so full he's almost sick. "No. No, I'm not, Mama. Me and Carl had . . . a parting of ways, I guess you'd say."

"That's too bad," his mother says. "I always thought he was such a pleasant man. Not a bit uppity. Always had time to stop and talk to you."

"I don't know, Mama. Carl changed. Got to feeling he was pretty important and all."

"Well, it's still a shame, especially when things was starting to work out so good."

"But that's all over now," he says, wanting her to get on to something else. "No big deal."

"But a partnership would have been nice," she says. "You have to admit that."

He rolls his eyes.

"What goddamn partnership?" His old man glances back and forth between them. "Never heard of no partnership."

"It wasn't nothing official," she says. "But they was talking about it real serious, him bringing Ronnie in fifty-fifty."

"For how much? Carl ain't no fool. He wouldn't *give* half his business to nobody."

She frowns. Ronnie Blue shrugs and says before her doubt can fully register: "I don't see what difference it makes now anyway, since I'm not there and talking about it just makes everybody feel bad. Besides, I got my eye on something else. Going to look into it soon as I get back. A small garage, little one-man place. The guy's retiring and wants somebody to take it over. He knows I'm interested, but before this thing with Carl blew up we never had much reason to get down to the nitty-gritty. I'm going to try to talk to him, though, and see what we can work out."

"Why, if that's what you're wanting to do," his mother says, confidence restored, "you should come on back here and open a place. There's only one garage in town—Tony down at Mid-American— and he's higher than a cat's back. Nobody likes him, he takes so long and don't seem to care much what kind of job he does. He wouldn't last six months with any competition at all."

"I don't know, Mama."

"And I can tell you right where your place ought to be: that old filling station just down here at the corner of the cemetery road. Why, it couldn't cost much, if anything, and it's right out there where everybody can see it."

"It's hard thinking about coming back, Mama. I've been gone a long time and, you know, say I did. Say I moved to Bartlett's Junction and opened a shop. What would I do besides work? And what would Charlene do? There ain't even a movie here or a good place to buy clothes. You drink a beer and everybody knows it. She's not used to that. She's never lived in a small town."

"The boy's right, Ardell," his old man says. "About that. It's asking a lot after he's been gone this long. Take a whole bunch of getting used to. For the both of them."

"Others is doing it. Young folks moving back, settling in. Reggie Moss and Paul Yost and Art Morgan. And how about John Klein? Silly me, I forgot all about him and he's the most important one. As far as Ronnie's concerned."

"Why do you say that, Mama?"

"Well, you was friends, wasn't you?"

"Yeah, we were. But that don't mean we ever would be again."

"Could be, though. And anyway there's others that—"

"Who, Mama? Reggie Moss? Paul Yost? Art Morgan? The grocer, the lawyer, the school superintendent? Those the ones you mean, Mama? And who would I be? The junkman's son come home to fix their fancy cars?"

"You'd be Ronnie Blue," she says, pulling herself so straight she's bent back, a sapling set to slap the next person by. "And Ronnie Blue's always been good enough."

"For me, Mama. And for you. But not for them. I am what I am and they don't forget. Like that night John Klein and me got drunk and my old man here called the cops on us? I was his best friend in the whole world then, Mama. But you know what? I ain't heard a word from him since. Not a goddamn word—pardon my French. That's what I'm talking about, Mama. That's why I got no desire to come back here. Later, maybe, when I'm rich—and I will be rich, Mama, I can tell you that. Then maybe I'll come back. I'll put all my money in John Klein's bank and say, 'John, you be nice now, you hear, or I'll take my money right back out.' And he'll be nice, Mama. I guarantee it. And Reggie Moss'll give me *my* food and Paul Yost'll be *my* lawyer and Art Morgan'll be superintendent for *my* kids. Me and Charlene'll buy Theo Klein's old house down on Spruce, and we'll fix it up nicer than any place in town and just set in it. No working. We're rich, remember. Nobody'll like it because we are, because we don't do nothing to make our money, but they'll want to know us anyway. They'll want to come and see us when we have a party—and we're going to have the best parties ever in this town. They'll all want to be there, Mama, lining up at the door, like at a big concert. But just the ones with tickets is going to get in. The rest of them'll just have to want. That's when I'm coming back to stay, Mama."

He takes a deep breath. He hasn't said so much so fast in months. And definitely not to so many people. Charlene is beaming, her foot caressing his knee. His mother's lips twitch, as if feeling out bones from a mouthful of fish. His old man stares, lids drawn down like flesh swollen around wounds. Nobody saying anything. Like they're waiting for more, for him, Ronnie Blue, to tell them the rest of what's on his mind.

6

*J*ohn Klein shakes his head. It isn't a flattering portrait—Wiley Bartlett in the late 1880s, shortly before he left town, a haggard man, with a bulbous alcoholic nose and a grey tinge to his cheeks, a man clearly marked for death. Yet there's something comic about it, too, as if the painter had caught Bartlett in the midst of telling a joke he realized no one would ever hear the punch line to. It's doubtful that he ever hung the picture, but being as vain a man as he was, he would have been unable to destroy it, either, hoping, as he must have, that people would one day forget Theophilus Klein, regardless of his good deeds, and that he would re-emerge dominant in the town's memory, that it would be his mark on history, his life and death that people cared about. Crooks and cranks always have been more interesting than people who just do their whole lives, and when the idea of a shrine to himself crossed his mind, including his likeness, particularly one with such a sneer, such a look of bemused contempt, it must have seemed to him a perfect final gesture.

What Wiley Bartlett could not have known, but would have appreciated, was that it would be Martha Klein who, soon after moving into his house in the fall of 1976, would discover the portrait where he'd left it, propped in a rocking chair in a boarded up section of the attic.

"Why, it was like opening a tomb or something," she said the first time he heard the story, a quiet evening he'd been invited for supper and to see something she thought might interest him. She'd gone to the attic on a whim, she assumed, to see what was there. It was gloomy and dusty and filled with junk. Generally uninteresting, she remembered, and she was about to leave when she heard a scratching sound. Afraid that squirrels or rats might be in the walls, she went to look. The noise was coming from one of two gables on the east side of the house. She found nothing to speak of in the first and the other, of course, was sealed off. But that was where the beast was, wouldn't you know, so she grabbed a crowbar which happened to be lying nearby and pulled a board loose. And that was all it took. She stopped dead in her tracks. She may even have let out a little eek or some such, she couldn't say for sure, because there she was in the attic for some reason she's never been able to explain quite satisfactorily, chasing an animal that may or may not have existed—it hasn't been seen or heard from since—holding a crowbar so conveniently placed it might as well have jumped into her hand—there she was, suddenly face-to-face with Wiley Bartlett.

"That was something, I'll tell you, him staring out from that rocker so life-like and all. Why, he could've talked and it wouldn't have surprised me. Not a bit. Now I wish he would have. It would've saved a lot of trouble if he'd just said then and there what to do with every-thing. But he didn't, of course, and I knew it wasn't right for me to make that kind of decision on my own—unlike some other people I could mention—so I left it just the way I found it and came on back downstairs to call Bud. Now isn't that what you would have done, John?"

"And I came right home, too, didn't I?" his father said. "As soon as I hung up. Couldn't have been more than ten minutes at the most. And the reason I did—now you have to understand this from the start—was because I was worried she was going to go back up there and mess around in that stuff. That would have been all right by me if we hadn't been dealing with a guy like Wiley Bartlett. He was crazy, you know. Not just neurotic, either, but out and out crazy. Why, who else would have done a thing like he did—and to his own people, too. People who trusted him, people some say even loved him. For a man in that kind of position to turn around just like that and stab everybody in the back—and I do mean *everybody* because he nearly sent this whole town under—to do that a man has to be crazy. Don't you think? So that's why I hurried home. I really wasn't sure what to expect. I had no more idea than anything what tricks he might've had up his sleeve. And I didn't want anybody getting hurt. You know what I mean?"

His mother sat patiently. On occasion she smiled or glanced at him so he'd be aware that there was more to the story than his father was telling. But she didn't interrupt. Neither of them did, each waiting for the other to finish, perhaps mouthing the final few words of the previous speech, like a cue before making an entry. It was obvious they'd been through the scene before.

"So anyway," his father went on, "as soon as I got changed, we marched up to the attic and started to work. We took off every board real slow and easy. Didn't want any surprises, if you know what I mean. And what we found was just amazing. You kind of have to use your imagination here, all right? First off, there's the gable. The triangle shape and all? Okay, and right in front's old Wiley in that rocker, looking like something the cats drug in. And behind him there's all this other stuff: big dark furniture, lots of books and papers and such, and a few old-time photographs. It looked just like any other pile of junk you'd see. But it wasn't. No, sir, not by a long shot. Because when I picked up that portrait to move it out of the way so we could get in there, the strangest darn thing happened—and this gives you a little more idea what Bartlett was like. When I moved that painting, the whole display sort of fell apart. Now I don't mean it crumbled or broke to pieces. It was more like without him, there really was just a pile of junk. Old junk, but still junk. So I put it back and—your mother'll even agree with me here—it all came together again into this—what should I say?" inclining toward his wife, but not waiting for her reply—"this picture, this *statement* about the town. How it was settled and grew and how he got together with Great-Grandpa Klein and all the things they did before he went nuts and stole the money. And it was real clever, too, the way he had it fixed, one thing building on the next and so on. You have to give him credit: he may have been a thief, but he was a sly one, there's no getting around that. Because he made sure nothing was going to make sense without him being there. He was directing all of it, you see? From that rocker. It was just like he was alive again."

And in a way he was. It was impossible to listen to the story and not look at the portrait; and looking at the portrait, it was impossible not to think of the man, Wiley Bartlett. Once he did that, he had to wonder at the workings of the brain that could have brought to play what he heard happening. In the silences that evolved, he could almost hear a distant, hollow laughter.

What they had uncovered that day, his mother said, picking up the story, was possibly the best find of Great Plains historical artifacts in the past thirty years—and maybe even in this century. Once they had all the things out where they could see them, they found quite a lot more than a pile of junk. There were three wardrobes of clothes;

several pieces of period furniture; a half dozen tintypes (one of which shows Wiley Bartlett and Theophilus Klein posing in front of the train depot, OXBOW STATION visible behind them); personal effects, such as a gold pocket watch, a razor, a place setting of silver, china and crystal; and a small library of newspapers, magazines, books, letters, diaries and journals. According to her, it was the kind of collection that was bound to bring State Historical Society people down from Topeka in droves.

His father, however, wasn't about to let them have it. They could look. They could drool. But that was it. As president of the Bartlett's Junction Discoverers Club, he had other plans. With his wife's agreement, the display would be moved intact to the old frame building which had housed the first free public library in the state and which now served as the Bartlett's Junction Museum, where he was also curator.

In the beginning, their arrangement seemed to be going smoothly. They appeared to be in perfect accord on what to do with what, where to put things to their best advantage and so on. But then something happened. Some snag developed which each blamed the other for. Exactly what it was wasn't articulated until later. His mother would say only that she'd had second thoughts. His father said he wished he'd never given her any control at all over the disposition of Bartlett's things, and surely wouldn't have had he known how she was going to carry on. But he had, in his first flush of excitement. He had actually told her she could do what she saw fit, since she had discovered the cache. His statement, of course, has proved an incautious one, quite unbankerly and quite unlike his father, for his assumption that she would follow his directions no matter what simply has not panned out.

In the end, she gave him everything but two brass lamps (which he had no desire for anyway)—and the portrait. She put the lamps in the den and the portrait over the fireplace. Temporarily, she said. Until certain conditions were met.

Her move was deliberate. She knew precisely the effect the missing portrait would have on the display, but she has held her ground, making clear to anyone and everyone that she is not merely engaging in silly, selfish shenanigans. She is intentionally withholding it, and will continue to do so. Unless, of course, she gets what she wants. Then she'll be more than happy to see the painting back in its rightful place.

"Tit for tat," she says, in what she calls her monkey-see, monkey-do defense.

"I've told you I don't know how many times that those papers got lost in transit," his father says.

"That's right, you have."

"And I feel as badly about it as you do."

"Of course."

"Because Wiley Bartlett's writings would have made an—*interesting*—addition to the town's history. And their absence—"

"Is a tragic loss for everyone," her voice just short enough of singsong that she can't be accused of ridicule.

"I don't think I'd use the word 'tragic,'" his father says, "since we can't really be sure one way or the other. Now, can we? They may, in fact, have only reconfirmed what we already know."

"But it still would have been nice if somebody had gotten to see them first," she says.

No answer.

"That way we'd at least have an idea what was in them."

"True, but—"

"Now it's worse than if we'd never known the papers existed. All we have left is questions. Speculations. Your grandfather's account of things. Not that what he said is necessarily wrong. I don't mean that at all. But I can't help being curious, either. Can you? I'd frankly like to know what Wiley Bartlett thought was important enough to go to all that trouble to tell us."

And there it ends, time after time, like being stuck on a dirt road, rocking back and forth over the same ground again and again, sinking slightly deeper with each passage.

But their argument hasn't always been so formalized and controlled. In fact, for the first year after they found the portrait, after the evening they told him about it, there was no argument. All they would allow themselves to discuss was *how* they'd made the discovery, and that with great relish to anyone who was polite enough not to say he'd already heard the story. Looking back, it's clear that his father still assumed she would eventually give him the picture, regardless—she'd never failed him yet in anything really important—while she, convinced that he was concealing information, had no intention of surrendering it until he produced the papers. So although their positions were set, they remained unstated, each perhaps recognizing that by addressing everything but the underlying problem, they could, for all intents and purposes, carry on life as usual.

Their truce ended the next spring, however. He'd brought Linda to the house for supper and afterwards they'd all gone to the patio for coffee. Linda had noticed the portrait before, but had never asked about it. When she did, his parents were happy to oblige her and began the story as they had dozens of times, building the suspense, relating in minute detail what they'd done and seen—all the while protesting that if Linda got bored, she was to let them know. Raise her hand or stamp her foot, anything but yawn, if she could help it. She smiled and assured them she wasn't in the least bored and please to go on with it. And she was sincere. She was obviously taken by the story and amused at his parents' telling of it.

He soon found himself drifting against the backdrop of his mother's and father's voices to thoughts of how much he liked Linda and being there with her, how he liked the looks of her calves and knees—even they seemed perfect—her bare arms and neck, how she'd made him laugh in spite of himself that evening on Miller's Hill, how she'd tasted and felt on the rocky ground.

Then he was sitting up, suddenly alert, as if someone had shaken him awake.

His parents had their arms locked across their chests. Their necks were bowed, brows lowered. They were glaring at each other. It was his father who finally spoke.

"Second thoughts. That's what she called them: second thoughts. Humph!"

"I had every right to change my mind and you know it."

"You could've at least talked to me first."

"I tried to. Dear god, I tried to."

"By accusing me of stealing."

"I did not."

"Oh, yes. You said it would've been impossible to lose those papers."

"I think I said it seemed 'improbable.' To me."

"And of course, then, by implication I'm also a liar."

"No. I don't believe you're capable of lying, Bud. Distorting the truth, maybe, because you can't help it, because in your mind there can be only one version of what happened between your grandfather and Wiley Bartlett."

"And that makes me an ogre?"

"All I'm saying is that history has to judge what Wiley Bartlett did. Not me. Not you. Not your family."

"It has judged him, and it found him guilty."

"Then what are you afraid of?"

"I'm not afraid. I'm sad. I'm weary. I feel betrayed when someone as close to me as you is willing to defend the likes of him."

"That's not fair."

"What is, Martha? When push comes to shove, what is?"

"You don't mean that."

"I most certainly do."

"You're telling me loyalty is worth more to you than love?"

"I can't separate them out like that."

"Oh. I see. I really do. Now. The reason you came home so fast that day wasn't to protect me at all, was it? You were afraid I'd find out something and you couldn't quite bring yourself to trust me, could you? I am only your wife, after all. Why, I could've had a whole quiver of poison arrows shot through me and that would've been more tolerable than if I'd read that stuff. Wouldn't it? Bud?"

"Yes."

And for the first time he could remember, they were yelling at each other: he was cruel, she was heartless; he was a fool, she was an idiot; he was contemptible, she was despicable. His father stopped just short of calling his mother a bitch, and she ran into the house in tears.

"Wow!" Linda said.

He shrugged and tried to laugh, but was too embarrassed. They left without saying goodnight.

Three days later his father called him at home before work, asking him to come by his office as soon as he got in. He sounded too bright, too cheerful. The way you talk when somebody's died.

"Come in, son."

Despite air-conditioning, the room was stuffy, oppressive; and "son" said in that tone of voice always made him sweat. First under the arms, then across his upper lip, a milk moustache without color.

"Sit down, sit down. Coffee?"

"No, thanks."

"I grabbed an extra sweet roll at Trudy's on the way over."

"I'm fine. Just finished breakfast."

"I hope you don't mind if I—"

"No, go right ahead."

His father poured himself a cup of coffee, added cream but no sugar, then meticulously unwrapped the sweet roll and cut it into sixths.

"We don't get to do this much, do we? Sit and talk, I mean. Just you and me. And it's a shame, too. Some of my fondest memories of your Grandfather Ephram are from times like this. We'd both be here early or something and before long he'd be in my office or I'd be in his. Just talking. It was kind of a way of keeping up with each other, I guess."

He tried to imagine Ephram Klein sitting where his father was, his father where he was. There would have been only one portrait then on the wall behind the desk. Theophilus Klein, painted from a photograph taken late in life, painted after his death because he believed portraits smacked of sinfulness. An old man without palsy, eyes dark and clear, sharp face stern and solemn. His son, Ephram, a near mirror image twenty years younger, and with a glint of mirth—or early madness—in his eye, trained now on his son, Bud, a still younger version of himself across the desk as they talked father to son to son, and now again to son. John Klein lifted his father to the wall and sat in his place behind the desk, talking to no one.

Finished with the sweet roll, his father refolded the wrapper and dropped it into the wastebasket. He brushed what crumbs there were into his palm and dumped them. He straightened his penholder, a stack of papers. He realigned his letter opener with the edge of the blotter and glanced to see that the door was still closed.

The small talk was over.

"That was quite a fracas the other night, wasn't it? I hope Linda wasn't too offended."

"She'll survive."

"She seems like a nice girl. She's easy to talk to and everybody I know just thinks the world of her. I believe she'll make you a good wife, if that's what you want."

"Thanks."

"You'll need that with what you've got ahead of you. You'll need somebody who'll stand by you and support you, who'll give you love and understanding, who'll trust that you're doing what you see is right even when it may not look that way to her."

"But I'll also want her to tell me if I'm getting out of line."

"Of course you will." His father dropped forward, shoulders square with the desk, a dark mahogany piece just right for him, in an office just right for the bank, just right for the town. To know what was just right was to survive. "But you'll be the one who has to make the decisions in the end, you see. You'll be the one who has to act because you'll be in charge. And once you've done something, she'll need to abide by it."

"Doesn't sound very democratic."

"In some matters you can't be." He pushed himself back, framed now by the two elder Kleins. For a moment they blended, eyes, noses, mouths one, his father then re-emerging in a softer voice, hands folded on his chest. "I know you think I'm wrong. Your mother thinks

I'm wrong. And I know you've talked to her since our—discussion—
the other night. What you said to each other is your business, I'll not
pry into that. All I want is for you to hear my side of this: I did take
the papers. They're in a safe deposit box registered in your name."

"Now wait a minute. You can't just—"

He held up his hand. "What your great-grandfather did was
totally selfless. It was an act of love. He could have taken his money
and run, too, you know, but he didn't, and I'll not have the memory
of him sullied by a pack of slanderous—" He stops, rights his shoulders, stares at some point above and behind his son's head and con-
tinues speaking in a calm, studied voice. "The point is he stayed, and
because he did this town is here today. God knows we could do with
more of that kind of goodness and decency. But instead we get less.
Every day there's less. So it's up to us. It's up to us as people—as
Kleins—to see that his story is preserved. Intact."

He opened the top right hand desk drawer, took out a small
manila envelope and emptied the key to the safe deposit box onto the
blotter.

"Take it."

"I don't want it."

"Take it, John. Son," the three of them fixing him in their stare.

He should have told his father to go to hell. But he didn't. Nor did
he take the key. Nor did he turn down his mother's invitation to
breakfast. He's not much happier with her the way she taunts his
father with Bartlett's portrait, telling everyone she's going to get rid of
it, but then leaving it in the most prominent place in the house. It's
inflammatory. It's senseless. He tried to tell her that, but she refused
to yield.

It's gotten so at times he wishes he'd never come back. He feels
cheated and used. It makes him angry every time he goes to their

house and sees the portrait and hears the argument cranking to life again. He's tired of it. He's sick of it. He can't stand listening to another word about it.

"For Christ's sake, will you just shut up and eat!"

His mother blanches, his father rocks back in his chair, Linda fingers the rim of her water glass.

Then it's she who saves them, as always, smiling, turning to ask his father if the flowers are from his garden. They're so beautiful she'd love to have some to take home with her, if he doesn't mind. And she also wants the coffee cake recipe, although heaven knows she doesn't need the calories. His mother says she wishes she had the same problem, the conversation slipping from there to bathing suits to the swimming pool to the opening of the new tennis courts to the carnival and all that each of them has to do before they can finally settle on the dry grass of the athletic field at dusk, waiting for the best fireworks display in the state—and maybe the finest anywhere—to begin.

They rise then, civilized, once again in possession of themselves, and go out to cut flowers.

7

Ronnie Blue opens the same window he always has. The one nearest the rear on the south side of the old Klein house. It's easy to get to because of the porch somebody added. But just there. Not on the front and not on the north. It had to have been Ephram. Theo wouldn't have had anything that unbalanced on his house. And Ephram was nuts; even John said that. Mostly toward the end, after his wife died. He lived alone in the place for years and years. Him and about a million cats. People say they yowled all night sometimes. They say he skinned them alive, even ate some of them, and kept their skeletons on a shelf in the basement.

When Ronnie Blue was a kid, the story was that the house was haunted, that if you just went in and sat and didn't do or say anything you'd begin to hear things, and if you stayed long enough you'd finally see things, too. So he started going in to find out for himself, to see if they knew what they were talking about. They didn't. He must have gone a dozen times and he never saw a thing. Once, around midnight, he heard a sound he was never quite able to figure out. Kind of a clanking, wheezing, scraping sound. But that was it. Only that one time. So it had to have been a tree limb or the old sewer gurgling or just a creaky house flexing its joints.

After word got around about what he'd been doing, people would come up to him—mainly kids—and say, "Is it *really* haunted, Ronnie?" He'd tell them they should go find out for themselves. But they'd just stand there a while, shuffling their feet and looking embarrassed. Then he'd tell them he'd go with them, if that's what they wanted. They always did. He'd wait at the window, holding the curtain back like a tour guide at some cave or something. When they were all in, he'd lead them around, upstairs and downstairs, the basement, and once they'd seen everything, he'd take them back to the tower. It wasn't a tower, really, but he called it that since it rose straight from the front door to a square notched top that made the house look sort of like a church and sort of like a castle. It's where the stairs were. Halfway up was a landing with a window. Under the window was a bench where he'd tell them to sit, because from there you could see and hear everything, including what was going on outside. By then they'd be pretty jittery, and all he needed to do to set them off was tell about the night he heard the noise. After that, shadows, rafters popping in the heat, a mouse scurrying along the baseboard—anything— would start them giggling and squealing and imagining who knows what.

He never took more than three people at once. It was best with somebody alone, but that was hard to do, especially with girls. He always figured they went in pairs for protection, probably not so much from what he might do as from what they might let him do. Everybody had the hots for Ronnie Blue, whether they knew it or not. Except the guys. They just laughed and poked each other when they got scared. But the girls wanted to get close—hug and cuddle and pretend to have shivers. It was easy to tell if that was all they wanted to do. Most of the time it was, but when it wasn't that was fine, too. He was willing to do just about anything short of burning the place down. The crazier the better, as far as he was concerned. Like the night Patty Blake wanted to take off her clothes and have him watch her dance and walk around and stuff. And she was as virgin as they come.

But the best time—and the last, really—was Halloween of his senior year. By then everybody knew about the house, and he told someone, he can't remember who, that they'd ought to have a party there. That was all it took. Halloween night thirty or forty people showed up, maybe more. It was hard to tell, since one of the catches was that they couldn't have lights. No candles or anything. Just the street lamp on the corner. But that didn't keep them away. Not at all. They just kept coming and coming and bringing more and more stuff. They had beer and punch spiked with a hundred and fifty proof grain alcohol, dope, all kinds of chips and nuts and sandwiches. Somebody even brought a battery-powered record player, and it was so loud and dark with everybody in their costumes getting drunk and stoned out of their minds, it was just a hell of a time. People laughing and dancing and fucking. You could see them in the corners, hear them in the bedrooms. It was a blast. He had one of the Whitman twins—he wasn't sure which—on the bench under the window on the landing. Backwards, her on top, her peasant skirt—she came as a gypsy—hiked up in the rear, her legs stretched down his, bare feet curled around his calves, pulling herself down, the front of her skirt fanned out over both of them. God, she had nice legs. She wasn't much to look at, but she had fine legs, long and lean and straight, and he remembers how smooth they felt that night, how they quivered and finally relaxed, coming back together as she snuggled up on his lap.

Somebody was laughing. At the top of the stairs. For some damn reason he called out: "Hey, Theo, that you?" Somebody else said: "Jesus, it is!" Then somebody screamed, somebody yelped and somebody said: "Get him!" It was a stampede, people thundering up and down the steps, along the hallways, outside, nobody stopping to look or ask questions, just shrieking and hollering to each other in the dark, chasing a ghost that wasn't there.

It might have gone on the whole night if Dewey Cole hadn't showed up. He stuck his head in the window and somebody handed him a drink. He came on in then and didn't do anything, really, except have a couple more glasses of punch. But just having him there in the middle of the room with his cop's uniform on made everybody a little nervous, and they started settling like chickens after a coon's been through, sitting around now as far out of sight as possible, blinking, wondering what all the excitement was, getting quiet. Finally Dewey said it looked like they'd been having a good party, but didn't they think it was about time to go home now?

And that was it. Everybody left. A week later there was a lock on the window, one he could pick with no problem. But it did the job. Nobody wanted to go in anymore. The lock made the house private property again.

It was stupid, an asshole thing to do. So what if they had a party there? Nobody hurt anything. They even went back and cleaned up, which was more than Bud Klein had done in twenty-five years. After his old man died, he was finished with the place. He didn't even have the lawn mowed, and you'd think he'd do that just to keep the neighbors from yelling.

So as far as Ronnie Blue was concerned, locked or not the house was up for grabs. And he took it as his retreat, his pad, his corner of the world. He practically lived there the rest of his senior year. But that's what you have to do, isn't it? Take what you want before somebody else does and you end up with nothing? You take it and make it yours.

Just like with people, eyeing the trough Charlene's dress forms between her legs as she sits on the window sill to swing her feet inside. The lift, the flash of bare thighs. She's his because he took her and made her his. She's his because he says she is.

"What do you think?" he asks, stepping in after her.

She stands in the middle of the living room, a hand on top of her new hat, as if to keep it from blowing off. "I don't know. It's kind of creepy."

"That's because everything's all covered up. Here." He yanks a sheet from a table. "Look at that. Beautiful, ain't it? You can't buy stuff like that anymore."

She walks slowly past draped pictures and furniture, her feet and dress leaving a trail in the dust. "It's still creepy. I mean, it's like he ain't really gone. Or if he is, he's coming back any minute now. You know?"

"That's silly."

"You asked me what I thought."

"Well, there ain't nobody here."

"Except us, you mean?"

"Except us."

"And we shouldn't be."

"Now don't start on that again."

"There was a lock on the window, Ronnie. You didn't tell me there'd be locks."

"But locks're just made to be unlocked, ain't they?"

"Unless you get caught."

"This ain't Wichita, Charlene. The most that'd happen around here is you'd have to explain to Dewey Cole what you were doing, and he'd just stand there and pick his teeth and grin at you."

"Well, anyway," she says, "I've seen it now. I'm ready to go."

"But you ain't seen nothing yet. Now, come on. We've got the upstairs and the basement and all the rest down here. Where you want to go first?"

"Out."

"Charlene! What the hell's got into you? You've never been like this before."

"Never been in a haunted house, either."

"It ain't haunted! How many times do I have to tell you?"

She crosses her arms as if chilled, eyes flipping past him side to side.

It's crazy. She's just like everybody else, scared in spite of what he says. He glances toward the stairs, thinking of the bench under the window, the Whitman twin, wondering whether it will be as good there this time as it was then.

"Come on," he says. "We'll make it fast."

8

$\mathcal{Y}$ou okay?" Linda asks.

"Yeah, I'm all right." John Klein leans against the steering wheel to see around the hedge at the end of the drive.

"I thought you'd lost it there for a little bit. I really did."

"Maybe I should sometime." He pulls slowly onto the road. "Maybe I should just get it all off my chest."

"What good would that do?"

"I'd feel better."

"And they'd feel worse," she says. "It's hard enough for them as it is."

He turns north down a gravel road that marks the west edge of Klein property. They pass his father's trench silo which gives off the sour-sweet scent of rotting silage, his father's hay field where once he nearly suffered sunstroke bucking bales in a hundred and ten degree heat for the man who previously owned the land. They pass his father's prize herd of Black Angus cattle grazing lazily in the shade near Deever Creek. They cross a bridge with a wooden deck that isn't his father's and mount the embankment toward the Santa Fe tracks.

"I've been thinking about stealing the portrait."

"John!"

"Or maybe having somebody else do it. Then I'll burn it. I'll do that myself. Just stand there and watch it go up in flames."

"And all their—your—problems with it, I suppose."

Cedar, the easternmost street in town, is little more than a dirt lane. Dust rising behind them catches on the wind and drifts out over asbestos-shingled houses, tar paper shanties with sheets of plastic still tacked over the screens, trailer houses baking in the sun—all on great open lots that share a giant elm or two and a few spindly saplings, tethered as if to keep them from wandering off to a more hospitable climate. The grass is brittle, the ground cracked with fissures so large a bicycle wheel can wedge in them.

"You don't believe me, do you?" he says.

"I'd frankly rather not."

"Well, I've got to do something. It can't go on like this."

"I have an idea," she says, tapping her watch crystal. "Mrs. Mayhew left twenty minutes ago, you know."

"Do you ever think of anything else?"

"You should talk," her smile still holding.

"No, I mean it."

"Sure, you do."

"You've been on this ever since I picked you up."

"And?" Brows raised, she tilts her head as if talking to a particularly difficult student.

"It's just that there are other things in the world is all. Especially right now."

"Okay, I understand. We're adults. No big deal."

"Yes, it is," he says, the chatter of rocks on the fenders ceasing as they come to asphalt, black and soft, fumes mixing with cool air inside the car. "Look at you."

"And *listen* to you. I want you back from out there, John, from them. Please. This happens every time we go. They're there, we're here. And we've been looking forward to this all week, remember, going to my room because it would be fun there, because it would be funny? Well, we only have forty-three minutes."

"That old woman'll stand around and gab for an hour after church. You know that."

"But she might not, either, as unpredictable as she is."

"Aren't you the one who said taking the chance would be half the fun?"

"That's not the point, John."

"Okay, what is? What the hell is!"

"Go ahead, yell all you want."

"Linda—"

"We might as well sound like them, too."

He hunches over the wheel. She stares out the side window. They drive west now, heat shimmering from the street. West past the funeral home, Mrs. Gaul's, the hotel with rusty screens you can smell on a wet day, the bank corner. Traffic flows unbroken from the north and south, girls on the sidewalks in shorts and halter tops, boys ten feet behind, snickering. A beer can rolls to the gutter, a car backfires. They join the procession, funneled west between the post office and the electronics plant, onto a street lined with flags and old people on porches, past the Co-op elevator, the Rock Island tracks, down a long slope to the gates of City Park, the top of the Ferris wheel visible above the trees.

He turns right, driving a block north against traffic, and parks in the alley behind Mrs. Mayhew's.

The air in the car begins to warm.

"You're right," he says. "I've been an ass, and I apologize."

She smiles again, nodding—agreement or forgiveness or both, he can't tell—then glances toward the back door.

As they pass the trash cans lined up neatly along one side of the porch, he tries to imagine his father ever doing anything like this. But maybe he did. Maybe not here, in town, but somewhere, with someone. His mother? Some other woman he met? He's only human, as Linda would say. But how about now? Would he dare make love, even to his wife, in daylight? Isn't his life so standardized, so well-ordered that spontaneity would not only be difficult, but dangerous? And when did it happen? When did things begin to change? His pulse quickens as he follows Linda up the back stairs to her room, her fragrance, the movement of her hips emptying him for an instant, making him almost sad. There are moments, off moments when his mind says no one is watching, when he sees the shape of his father's hand in his own, hears his father's voice saying his words, notices his father's scalp on his head. And inside, in his brain, are his father's thoughts there, too? His grandfather's? His great-grandfather's? In ten years will he be wearing Klein clothes, living in a Klein house, teaching a fifth generation Klein son the virtues and rewards of living the Klein life?

Closing her door with her foot, she kisses him. "John. My dear, dear John," hugging him, hands stroking his neck and back, the nearly imperceptible tremble of her fingers betraying in her the same fear, the same sense of entrapment he feels. Only she will always be more free to leave than he. A cold weight drops inside him, and he holds her, squeezes her, presses her to him, until she pushes him away, backing him toward the bed.

He sits awkwardly, boyishly, while she undresses. He has savored the same performance at his house, there enjoying the slowness, the sauciness and suggestiveness. But in this house, Mrs. Mayhew's house, he is so aroused he can't wait.

Flinging his clothes aside, he makes a space for her, and she comes to him. And here in this virginal room, its blue-flowered wallpaper coordinating with blue curtains, the white bed and dresser, Linda's skin and veins, here with the only woman he has ever loved, amidst the senseless repetition of the merry-go-round's recorded calliope, the peals of joy from the swimming pool across the street, he parts her legs and makes ready his escape.

The house shudders, a door clattering against a stop.

"Yoo-hoo! Anybody here?"

Linda tenses.

"To hell with her," he groans, in her now, holding her with all his might.

"Yoo-hoo! Is that you, Linda?"

"It's my fault," she says. "I left the door unlocked. She'll be scared to death."

"Good. Then we won't have to worry about her."

"She's just an old woman, for pity's sake." She shoves at him. "Come on, I have to get up. I have to talk to her, John. You know that."

He lets her go, staying in bed himself, naked on top of the sheets, daring someone to find him, a dull, familiar ache radiating through his groin as he rolls toward the window and closes his eyes against the light.

9

$\mathcal{I}$'m sorry," Charlene says. "I really am."

"Yeah, yeah." Ronnie Blue's face is pressed to the circle rubbed in the grime on the tower window. He has a full view of the street for a block in either direction, and of the walk from the house to the curb which intersects the main sidewalk to form a cross, weeds stiff and dry as boar's bristle around it.

"It must be doing it here," she says. "That must be what's wrong."

His eyes swing level with hers. "Fucking is fucking, that's all. Don't matter where you do it."

She shrinks away, a little girl in her hat, underwear wadded in fists tucked beneath her chin. Except she's too old to be a little girl. She knows too much, looks too tired.

He peers back out the window. Cars idling by pause, a flicker of brake lights as they pass his Chevy. Old women done up in clown-red mouths and cheeks suddenly remember and, fingers pointing, lips parting to yak, yak, yak like crows in a corn field, they glance from his car to the path he and Charlene broke through the weeds.

"Look there, it's Ronnie Blue," they're saying. "He's back. The boy's back."

A big blue Olds stops, air-conditioner water dripping on the pavement. Albert Dobbs waves at the driver and totters down the steps from his porch across the street. Arms braced on the top of the car door, his head wags up and down, like one of those silly toy ducks over a glass of water. Then the head lifts, stays, cloudy eyes squinting up at the sky.

They aren't talking about the weather. Ronnie Blue mashes his face against the glass, knowing how dusty, deathly his flesh will appear, but doubting that Albert Dobbs can see that far. What he should do is throw open the window and say, "Hey, Al, how the hell are you? Long time no see. What's that? Oh, yeah," pulling Charlene into view. "Me and my woman here, we're just having us a quickie to get the day off on the right foot. You know how it is." Closing the window with a wink, leaving him to stand in the street, his worn out old heart gushing with envy.

The Olds trembles. Albert Dobbs straightens, turns toward his house. He slips sideways at the exact moment the Olds does, its rear end whipping toward the curb, coming back into line, as if the pavement has been smeared with butter, both setting off again then, more slowly, with greater concentration.

"And anyway it's not all my fault," Charlene is saying. "I told you right from the beginning—"

Ronnie Blue jumps up, angry, skin prickly from heat, from nerves. "And I told you there wasn't nothing to be scared of, didn't I? And did you listen? Hell, no! Well, let me say it just one more time then: This is my place. I'm King of the Mountain here, and what I say goes. There ain't nothing to be scared of, for no reason. You got it now?"

A stutter step halfway up the next flight of stairs and back down. He has to move. He has to keep moving. If he stays still, whatever it is that drags this place, this town down will get them, too, hold them fast while it turns them into mush, into some damn heap of slime that'll get shoveled out with the rest of the shit. Keep moving. Keep doing. It's his day, even if it isn't going the way he planned it. Even if she is being a bitch. Even if he can't stand the goddamn heat, his old man and his old lady and that pile of goddamn junk they live by. It's his day and nobody's going to take it away from him. It's his day and he'll by god enjoy it. And so will she. No more crying and tensing up and telling him she can't, she can't, freezing him out like that. It's his day. He's damned if he's going to just sit around and disappear like Albert Dobbs or whoever the hell else. You can't stop. You have to keep going. Moving. MOVING. Ronnie Blue and the good old U. S. of A., too.

"Come on!" He yanks her by the arm, her head snapping back, eyes frightened. "Let's go!"

She stoops to get her underwear.

"Leave it!"

"But—"

"Just leave it!"

"All right, Ronnie, sure. Whatever you say."

She's holding back, like a fish on a line. A turtle. A dead weight. He drags her through the window, not bothering to close it.

Weeds whip them, thistles stinging their legs. Shingles litter the ground, nails sticking up like fangs, tar paper air, dust and pollen thick as gnats.

"Jesus!" She tries to hold herself off the seat, but can't, grimacing as the backs of her legs and hips sink onto hot vinyl.

The engine rumbles, erupts, burnt oil exhaust, the smell of baked canvas closing over them, floating off on the wind.

He kicks down the idle and leans toward Albert Dobbs, as impassive as some bleached out log washed up on his porch.

"How the hell are you, Al? Me and my woman here, we're finished now and won't be back for a while, so you can tell Bud Klein he can close up again, if he wants to," arm hung over the door raising in a sassy wave as they drive off.

Up and down, north and south: Spruce, Locust, Oak, Cottonwood, Euclid, Sycamore, Maple, Beech, Elm, Cedar. Then back and forth, east and west: South Street, First, Second, Third, Fourth, Fifth, Sixth, Seventh, Eighth, Ninth, Highway 50. Pacing, treading with no place to go, houses and the people in them as bland as the street names, but unable to stop, captive to the rhythm of their lumbering bear gait.

10

"Crazy," John Klein says, crossing the street from Mrs. Mayhew's to the park. "That woman is plain crazy."

Linda shrugs.

"She's so spaced she never did figure out what was going on."

She takes his arm. "I told her you were sleeping, that you'd been so busy you just had to have a nap."

"We could've stayed up there the whole day screwing and she would've thought the bed springs were birds singing."

"I like that idea," she says. "And it was going well, wasn't it? After we finally got started."

"Yeah, well, maybe it's best we don't go into that right now."

"Maybe so."

"It's a little too much—"

"Exactly," she said, squeezing his hand.

"You didn't let me finish."

"I'm sorry."

"Right, like I'm supposed to believe that."

"No, really."

"What I was going to say is that what happened is like the story of my life." He holds his hands up, framing the dusky green backdrop of trees. "You know: here lies a man who died of good intentions."

"Which is far better than having none," she says.

He stops them on the sidewalk beside the swimming pool. "I love you."

She smiles.

"I love you so much I'm going to kiss you right here."

She glances at the fence around the swimming pool where several teenagers stand watching.

He pulls her to him. She wiggles and twists, trying to free herself. Several more kids have joined the first few, summer brown and dripping, inside the swimming pool fence.

"No," she says. "Stop."

"Why are you making such a fuss over a little kiss?"

"Right," one of the kids says. "Go on, kiss him."

"Kiss him," another says.

"Yeah, kiss him," a girls says, hiding her braces with the back of her hand.

"Kiss him, kiss him," they chant. "Kiss him."

A car has stopped at the curb, the man and woman inside craning to see what the excitement is.

"Kiss him, kiss him," a tall kid's long arms marking cadence.

"All right, all right," Linda says, and everyone falls silent. She pecks him on the cheek.

"Noooooo!"

She steps back a moment then throws her arms around his neck, mashing her mouth on his, bruising his lip.

"Yaaaaah!" Whistles and catcalls and applause as she drops away and pulls him through the hedge after her.

"Don't you ever do that again," she says, the cheering and honking dying down now that they are out of sight.

"You loved every minute of it."

"I mean it," she says.

Laughing, he reaches for her.

"No. It's not going to be that easy now that I know your real intentions," she says and takes off running.

He watches, waiting until she passes the first picnic table, to set out after her, finally catching up at the new tennis courts, where they rest, fingers hooked through the fence.

"Are you still mad?" he asks.

"Some."

He slides his hand over her hip. "It's all Mrs. Mayhew's fault, you know."

"You really don't get it, do you, John?"

He shakes his head. "I guess not."

"I mean, I'm not a—" She sighs, stares in at the courts a moment and says, "They're beautiful. You should be proud."

"I am, but—" She puts her finger to his lips to silence him and he lets her, settling beside her, head to her shoulder, thinking how it was he chose this site for the courts. Location was part of it—a north/south clearing surrounded by giant American elms that receives constant sunlight, at least in summer, and no matter how windy it may be elsewhere, filters only the most modest breezes through the trees. But even more important to his decision was that as a child, he used to come here to read or just lie in the grass and stare at the sky and be at peace. It was his place and his alone, he felt, and he shared it with no one. Until it came to him that that was where he wanted the new tennis courts to be built. Why, he wasn't sure, since there were a half dozen other sites that would be as suitable and even then why tennis courts and not a gazebo or a rose garden? He didn't even play the game but did have the notion that any community worth its while needed tennis courts. And not just any old courts but the best they could put up.

He felt so strongly about project—unreasonably so, some, including his father, said—that for two and a half years he personally supervised every detail of their planning, financing and construction. Nothing was to be spared. Not time, nor energy, nor money. He wanted only the best and would hear of nothing less. He even went so far as to establish a trust fund adequate for the maintenance and eventual expansion of the courts, should the need ever arise. And with that they became self-supporting and self-perpetuating.

But it was worth the effort and criticism, he thinks, gazing now with Linda at that perfect cool green and rust expanse, the crisp white lines, the rippling nets. The truth is, the courts were finished a week ago, but he couldn't bring himself to open them for play. He wanted them to be unsullied for the first match—no ball marks, no streaks from the toes of tennis shoes, no broken glass, no cigarette burns. After that, everyone will be invited to play. After the match, the courts will officially become public property.

"So what are you planning to say?" she asks.

"I don't know." He eyes the four chairs set up on the center court—one for Bob Babcock, who will give the invocation, two for Dick Wall and Peter Lundstrom, the local regionally ranked tennis players who will compete in the dedication match, and one for himself.

"But you must have some idea," she says.

"Not really. Nothing I've written down anyway. There'll be a prayer like there always is and I suppose I'll tell a couple of jokes then and introduce Dick and Peter and make some remarks about why we went to all the trouble to build the courts in the first place. But beyond that, I haven't really thought about it."

"Are you nervous?"

"A little but not much." Something will come. It always does. And he pauses a moment, remembering how such an attitude used to bother him, but shakes it off and leans against the fence, her, listening to the whooping of children on the tilt-a-whirl and Ferris wheel, the distorted music from the merry-go-round and pony ride, the "stepradup stepradup, see wadjakinwin forda pretty lady dere, stepradup," chatter of the barkers floating over the empty bleachers opposite them, the bare courts, the now constant rat-a-tat-tat of firecrackers weaving like a thread through the other sounds, drawing them together.

"Anyway," he says, "you know as well as I do that around here you can't sound too fancy or people won't listen."

"Maybe so, and that's okay as long as you don't do that hat in your hand, talking to your boots kind of thing."

"You sound mighty uppity, lady."

"I intend to."

He smiles. She smiles. He kisses her lightly on the cheek.

"Want a hot dog?"

11

Ronnie Blue directs traffic around the dirt track at the park. People cruise it looking for a parking space to squeeze into or to see who there is to be seen. And they all notice him. And they all notice Charlene beside him, wind molding her dress to her body, a faint triangle of hair visible between her legs. It turns him on to think about no underpants and people ogling when they go by. A few stop long enough to say hello and get a better look. Friends. People he knew a while back. He can't remember all their names.

"Hey, Blue."

"Hey."

"Where'd you get something like that?"

"Eat your heart out."

"That ain't all I'd like to eat."

"Move on, you're blocking traffic."

And they drive off laughing, swigging beer, making grab-ass motions out the window.

They love him.

He needs to piss.

The feeling passes in the heat, the dust. He waves on car after car, the sound of one radio fading into the next, engines pinging, fan belts squealing, faces floating slowly by. "I'm Ronnie Blue, how do you do? I'm Ronnie Blue, how do you do?" A mechanical arm going out, raising. People paying their respects.

"Let's go," Charlene's voice nags, tinny and distant, like an old-time record. "I'm hot. I'm tired. I'm thirsty."

He points toward his car.

"Not that. I want something else. At least something to put it in. I drink any more straight, I'll get sick."

He sees for an instant chunks of egg, bacon and toast suspended in a pile of clear gelatin melting into the dust at his feet.

"Yeah," he says, his own stomach unsettling. "Yeah, let's do that."

They got the whiskey from his old man. Up the lane along the back of the junkyard, crouching with their heads just below the level of the grass, taking the top off the fill tank of an old American Standard toilet, not the slightest clunk or chink—he's seen his old man spray the whole damn place with buckshot just at the thought of somebody stealing his hooch—lifting out an almost full quart of Southern Comfort, and running like hell.

It went down well. In the first fifteen minutes he drank enough to put him on his ass. But it didn't. He didn't feel a thing the entire northern loop they took back into town. Except her cunt. She let him put his hand there. On top of her dress, like they were eight year olds or something. He could do whatever he wanted, as long as he didn't try to get her dress up. By the time they turned back south toward town, she was so hot she was trembling, but she still wouldn't let him in. He just couldn't figure what was with her and let her go. She could work it out on her own. He took the bottle and drank.

Between the two of them, it was half empty when they came to the gates of the park. But he still wasn't getting much of a buzz on.

He was pissed. This was supposed to be a fun day. He wasn't having fun. He couldn't even get drunk.

He felt like telling people where to go, so he directed traffic. Until she started in.

"Cotton candy and a Coke," Charlene says, stumbling as they cross the track, then nodding in agreement with herself. "Yep, cotton candy and a Coke."

She's the one who's drunk. Hell, somebody could rip her dress off and fuck her on the spot and she wouldn't care. Might not even know it. Unless it was him.

Holding her hat on, she wobbles up the embankment on the other side of the track and over thick electrical cords twisting like snakes through the yellow grass. Bees hover around a trash barrel. A young girl shrieks between them, a boy wetting her bare brown back with a water pistol.

The carnival isn't nearly as big as he remembers. Maybe ten canvas booths on one side, another ten or fifteen across from them, a couple of concession stands, a Ferris wheel at the far end with the tilt-a-whirl, the merry-go-round, the pony ride and a small roller coaster. Cheap. The booths filling with wind, grey dust, blowing out hot dogs and sugar, grease and sweat.

A sun-darkened woman sells cotton candy in a white trailer, her denim apron stiff and shiny where she has leaned against the machine. Her black hair is tied back in a red kerchief, flinty eyes sweeping the crowd behind him as she twirls a cone around the bowl. A fly crawls the underside of the glass.

"Dollar," she says, still not looking at him.

"I want a Coke, too."

"No Cokes."

"I want a goddamn Coke."

"Over there. Next."

"What the hell kind of a place—"

Her eyes swing to a guard standing nearby, who hitches his belt, night stick hard as a horse's dick dangling down his leg. The guard looks at Ronnie Blue.

"Goddamn gypsy," he mumbles to Charlene, backing away. "She's a goddamn gypsy just like the rest of them. Oakies and Arkies and gypsies."

The guard locks his arms behind his back, rocks forward on his toes.

"And that son of a bitch, I don't know where he came from."

His mother told him two years ago that the city council had decided to hire extra guards for the Fourth to help keep the crowds under control. Out of towners—kids mainly—who started tearing things up, setting fires in the streets and such as that. Either they hired guards or shut the whole works down for good. But he can't see why they had to go and get horse dicks from Newton and Hutchinson, or wherever. A bunch of goons nobody knows. At least if you get into trouble with Dewey Cole you can sit down and have a swig and talk about it, and it'll be over with. But not with these bastards. Why, they'll use those goddamn things and talk later. He knows. He's seen them on TV and what then? What'll happen when they start swinging?

"My Coke," Charlene says, as if only just remembering she wanted one. "Where's my Coke?"

He takes her by the hand, not sure she's sober enough to follow otherwise, and cuts across the flow of people to the Coke stand. She leans against the red wall beside him, tearing off pieces of pink fluff and eating them, sucking her fingers clean. She looks dazed, as if she's not seeing anything, her mouth a sticky round hole in her face. It's no

damn fun being with a drunk if you're not drunk yourself. And he
should be, and it pisses him off all the more that he's not.

Now that she has her Coke, she wants to ride the tilt-a-whirl.

"You'll get sick."

"Mawright." She wavers, the effects of the whiskey becoming
stronger the more time that passes.

He shrugs. "It's your stomach."

They amble by the booths, barkers measuring her tits and ass, his
hand and eye, their faces all the same dark mask. Only their terms are
different: three shots for a half dollar, four balls for a buck. Dime a
shot. You always win something. He wants to stop and shoot ducks
that revolve by on a chain in a trough. He always has been good at
that. Once the guy told him to leave, he was breaking the bank. But
Charlene, waving the empty cotton candy cone like a baton, moves
him on toward the rides.

While they wait in line, she finishes her Coke. She burps, swal-
lows.

"You sure you want to do this?" he says.

"Nothing to it."

She gets on, settles in the seat, giving it a couple of practice swings.
The diesel accelerates. The platform spins, changing the angle of its
tilt as it goes, each seat revolving independently on top.

She grins and waves, disappears down a slope. He turns away,
watching girls, an especially nice one with long tan legs bending over
a counter to toss rings onto pegs, her shorts pulling up tight enough
that they hang on the crescents of her hips when she straightens. He
wonders how far the tan goes, and if it doesn't stop, how it got that
way, and what it would take for him to find out.

Shrieks, shuffling bodies, the diesel shutting down.

"Oh, shit!"

"Yuck!"

"Jesus!"

"Get back, get back!"

The platform coasts to a halt. The operator goes around to the other side.

A little boy peers at the ground just in front of the fence.

"Is that puke, Mommy?"

"Yes, Joey," wiping at her blouse with a tissue.

"Yucko puke. Right, Mommy?"

"Shut up, Joey."

The operator leads Charlene to the gate. She sees Ronnie and lurches toward him, people standing clear to let her through. She's pale and frightened, a pink stain in the lap of her dress.

She says nothing, he says nothing as he walks her to a restroom. She pauses at the door.

"You hate me, don't you?" still slurring, still unable to keep her balance. "Made a fool of myself. All those people, they see you with me. I puked on them, Ronnie. Just like that."

"I know. Go on, clean up."

"Can't you even tell me it's okay, you love me anyway?"

"Go on in."

"Goddamn it, Ronnie, I puked on them." She holds herself in the doorway, squinting as if trying to make out his face in the light.

"So now they'll have something to remember you by."

She sinks away into the shadow and he hikes himself to the top of the rock wall beside him. Below are long rows of green bleachers. Then the football field where he never played football. Then the baseball diamond where he never played baseball. Then the park gates, cars streaming in the left side and out the right. Cars everywhere. The air thick with dust and heat and noise.

He can't remember why he wanted to come. Why he wanted to be here instead of staying home. Wouldn't have seen his old man and his old lady, wouldn't have had to go through that. Wouldn't have had Charlene being pissed and weird all day. Wouldn't have had her puking. Would have been in her pants. Would have fucked her head off. Would have had old Zimmerman down for some beers. Would have fucked some more, gone somewhere to eat, snuck into a drive-in, fucked until she begged him to stop.

Ronnie Blue and the good old U. S. of A., too.

Applause. Loudspeaker applause. Somebody talking.

". . . special day . . ."

". . . privilege and an honor . . ."

". . . long years . . ."

". . . for the people of Bartlett's Junction . . ."

Words and echoes bunching, scattering through new applause, waiting at the end of a phrase for the air to clear of sound. He'd know that voice anywhere.

He grabs Charlene by the arm as soon as she comes out and retraces their path through the crowd, the snaked cords, the traffic.

John Klein's back is to them as he gathers chairs, unplugs the microphone, clears the courts for the players, trim and tanned and dressed in white clothes with colored stripes, who wait at the far end, bouncing yellow balls with their racquets.

John Klein.

He turns. His eyes meet Ronnie Blue's.

Without looking away, he leans close to the man in the chair by the net.

"Take your seats, please," the man announces. "Everyone in your seats."

Meaning them. Him and Charlene. Everybody else is in the stand.

John Klein in the front row by a woman. Pretty. Nice legs. He smiles at her. She smiles at him. Nice teeth.

Mr. Bigshot. Mr. Banker.

"Your seats, please."

Son of a bitch.

12

*J*ohn Klein is basking in glory. There's no other way to say it. He's beaming. All the people around him are beaming. Talking. Celebrating. They love him. Linda loves him. He loves them. All of them.

His father seeks him out after the tennis match. He says nothing, really. Shakes his son's hand, claps him on the shoulder. Hugs him. He knows. He understands what it all means for his son and the community, his son in the community, and he approves.

His mother has tears in her eyes. But she is happy. And so proud.

Ed Neher, for whom the world is divided into those who work and those who don't—worth assigned accordingly—shoves his hat back on his head and sets the heels of his boots against the bench in front of him as he leans forward and says: "Now them boys playing that game, they put out down there today. That's for damn sure. They sweat, sure enough. You could see it all over them."

Even as little as a year ago, John Klein would never have heard those words. Not for candy-ass tennis players. This is football country. People here know tennis only through television, if that. He doubts that more than a handful of them have ever seen a live match. And television doesn't allow sweat. Not real sweat that soaks and stinks. Television allows Wimbledon and the U. S. Open. Glamour matches that perpetuate the image of tennis as a game played by rich, lean and sometimes naughty men who off-court probably wear sandals.

But today that's all been changed. They'll never again view the game the same way. Even on television.

It was a short match. He'd suggested three sets instead of five. Because of the heat. Because of time. Dick Wall and Peter Lundstrom agreed.

They played perfectly on perfect courts. Dick Wall finally won 6-4, 4-6, 7-6, but not until the last serve of the tie-breaker—which, incidentally, was an ace. It was great fun, great entertainment. The crowd oohed and aahed at the right times. They argued points, objected to line calls, remarked on the speed and agility of the players, their endurance. They became so taken by the rhythm and intensity of the match that once it was over, they were reluctant to give it up.

After Dick Wall's winning serve, when people realized the match was over, they applauded. They cheered. Someone stood. Then everyone stood, including Ed Neher. Dick and Peter waved. The crowd cheered louder yet.

Linda said they wanted him now; they wanted John Klein. He should acknowledge them. He glanced up the stand behind him. Nodded and grinned.

He took two steps out, spread his arms and said thanks. No one heard him. They didn't need to. They knew.

He was home now.

13

*P*link.

Aim.

Plink.

Nothing concerns him but the kill. Not the noise of the crowd. Not Charlene. Not the wooden-faced barker beside him fondling coins in his change apron. Only the kill.

Aim. Squeeze.

Plink.

The duck snaps over. Another takes its place.

He's been hitting ninety percent. At least. Nobody's better. He's dead on target.

The barker pushes away, jarring the counter.

Poooh. He misses the only shot he has to make. The prize shot. An empty sound, full of air. Son of a bitch can't stand to lose.

"Try again?"

"No, Ronnie!" Charlene says.

"Another chance?"

"You're a fucking cheat and you know it, mister."

"Don't wanna playda game, move on."

He puts down his dollar.

"Ronnie!" Like a fly you can't get rid of. Brush it away and it comes back. No matter what.

Sweat trickles down his left cheek. He wipes it, sets himself, aims. *Plink.*

The bastard'll let him go. Right to the end. They all do. Lead you on. Make you think you're doing great. Right to the critical point. Right to the point they stand to lose. The ring toss, the milk bottle game, darts, roulette, all of them the same. To win, you have to know when they're going to cheat. And how. So you can cheat them. Cheat the cheaters. Figure out their game and do it better than they do. That's the real chance you take when you lay your money down.

Plink.

Two things his old man taught him: if you want something, take it or somebody else will; and how to shoot.

Mad dogs in the junkyard. Whether they were there or not.

Once they were. A couple of rabid mongrels out by the appliances. His old man was scared. Sweating. Trembling. He'd never seen his old man scared before and it scared him.

They killed the dogs. But for a long time afterwards, he woke up screaming in the middle of the night.

He was supposed to flush them. Banging on refrigerators and freezers and washers and dryers with a baseball bat, he was supposed to drive them back around toward his old man. Who stood on a freezer out of harm's way. Who said not to worry, he was covering him. Mad dogs were to be pitied, you know. *They* couldn't even tell when they were going to attack.

The first one showed around the corner of a Frigidaire side-by-side. Half back on his haunches. Yapping. Yapping. Teeth bared, mouth flecked with foam, shaving lather left on too long. Eyes crazy, rolling. Not focusing on anything.

His old man got him with one blast. Knocked him over like a stuffed doll. He didn't make another move, another sound.

But while they were looking, the second dog outflanked them, came in from his right side. Growling. An angry, guttural, strangulating growl.

When she leapt, it wasn't at him, but past him. At his old man. The gun came up. Like a reflex. For a moment the barrels pointing directly at his face, then following the dog's flight.

Blood and hair and flesh rained on him.

In his dream the gun doesn't fire. The dog knocks his old man from the freezer. They disappear behind it. Snapping and snarling. Terrified cries. Tormented cries. He rushes to help, the bat gone. He grabs the dog by the throat, trying to pull her off, trying to control her. He can't look at his old man.

"Poor bastards," Chester Blue said, cutting the dogs' heads off to send to the state lab. "You just have to put them out of their misery, that's all."

Poor bastard, he says in his dream.

Ever after, they practiced on mad dogs at the back of the junkyard. *Mad dog!* his old man would yell. *Mad dog!* And they would fire. And they would kill it.

Plink.

Mad dog.

Plink.

Mad dog.

A hand on his shoulder. His old man telling him there are places to shoot and places not to shoot, and windows are one of the places not to shoot and he's going to beat his ass to make sure he remembers.

Mad dog.

Poooh.

"You son of a bitch!"

"Ronnie!" Charlene is at his side.

"Put it down, boy, put it right down." The mask at the end of the barrel empty but for the sound of a voice, a hand slipping from the coin apron to a trouser pocket. "Better put it down or you'll wish you had."

Maybe that'll teach you, boy. Maybe that'll teach you to use your head.

"Ronnie! Come on."

"You're a goddamn cheat. A crook."

She tugs. He moves.

The barker takes the gun, lays it down, turns to the next customer.

"He's a goddamn gypsy. Watch him, mister. Watch him like a hawk."

"Move along." A horse dick cop with a moustache steps between him and the booth.

"Ain't me. It's that son of a bitch. Cheating everybody that goes up there."

"That's enough, now."

"Come on, Ronnie."

"Watch him." He cranes around the cop. "Like I told you."

Plink.

Plink.

"Even then you won't win."

Poooh.

"Stepradup."

She's walking too fast. The air is too hot to breathe. The cop, arms folded across his chest, recedes behind them like a guard at a gate.

"Where're we going?"

"Away. I don't care. Just away."

"But you saw it, didn't you? You saw what was going on."

"Sure I did. And so did everybody else."

"Then why—"

"Because that's just the way it is, Ronnie."

Crossing the track to his car, he glances over at the tennis courts, vacant now except for a couple of kids swinging racquets too big for them.

"Not if you're John Klein, it ain't. Nobody would've kicked him out. Hell, no. If you are somebody or you know somebody, they always give you the last shot."

14

Even your once in a lifetime fifteen minutes of glory is like a toe-curling orgasm or food so good you don't want to swallow—and a sinking feeling that nothing can be that fulfilling without complication.

And usually it isn't. When you look at it, think about it, you'll find something. Compromise, guilt, too much pepper. Ronnie Blue's face through the chain link fence. The woman with him.

On their backs near the precipice of Miller's Hill, a bottle of "Chateau Gallo" beside them, he and Linda peer into the clear blue space directly overhead, where the sky seems to have cleansed itself of the dingy haze clouding the horizons. A lone hawk soars into view, floating as if on the surface of a crystal pool. It drifts a while longer before, wings folding, it dives to the prairie floor.

They were like refugees, their faces pressed to the fence, fingers hooked through it. Like displaced, homeless people looking for somewhere to go, but so down and out they don't recognize asylum when they see it.

Or maybe it's just easier to think that. Then he can believe he had no part in their leaving. Then he can believe that when the umpire called for everyone to be seated he expected them to come around and join him and Linda and that he would have moved Art and Kay Morgan down to make room. Room for Ronnie Blue, who was even dressed out of time, like a '30s gangster. Room for him and his friend with the stained dress and no underpants.

He can believe anything he wants because they left. They turned and walked away.

"I'd be mad, too," Linda says. "You didn't wave, you didn't nod. You didn't even act like he was there. How would you feel?"

"Relieved."

"Nonsense. Turn things around and it'd be a different story."

"Maybe."

"He's a friend, John."

"Was."

"A best friend."

"Five years ago," he says. "Things change. People change."

"Not always."

The hawk is back. Or another just like it, bobbing and weaving through currents of air.

"Does he embarrass you?" she asks.

"Maybe, I don't know."

"Will I embarrass you someday?"

He tries to explain about Ronnie Blue. He tells her how they became friends in the first place. About the cars and the singing and the drinking and fooling around. He tells her how they were so thick because neither of them had anybody else, how they knew if they ever parted for long at all they would probably never get back together. And when that time came how they just let it go. Not a word. He didn't even call the night before he left for college, and Ronnie Blue was the only person he cared to say goodbye to.

How suddenly five years were gone, and just as he'd thought, they hadn't seen or heard from each other the whole time. They'd heard *about* each other, he supposes, since it's impossible not to here. And he hasn't exactly forgotten Ronnie Blue, either; but in the meantime he has made new friends, he's started a new job, he has new things to do and look forward to.

And now along comes Ronnie Blue again. In the flesh. With his woman. And it's like time has stopped, backed up. He remembers so well how that car always smelled hot, clean hot, hotrod hot, how the ridge on the seat left red marks on the backs of his thighs. He remembers being drunk, driving ninety, wondering why he wasn't dead. He remembers whores and the Whitman twins, who were game for anything (which he doesn't recall for Linda). He remembers wind in his hair and stars and shooting the moon the length of Main Street, and thinking how much better it would be to have a notoriously drunk old man who spent half his time killing phantoms in the junkyard than to have the self-appointed protector of morality and family pride that he got stuck with.

But what he doesn't remember is how to act the way he did then, how to talk. And what's more, he doesn't really want to. That part of his life is over. Finished.

"And, I don't know, Linda, maybe if I could just say hello and goodbye and be sure that'd be the end of it, that there wouldn't be a bunch of loose threads left hanging, I'd go find him right now and we'd all sit down and yuck it up and go on about our business. But it doesn't feel like that. There's too much garbage in the way. I mean, when I saw him this morning in that same car with the same kind of woman he's always had, looking the same as ever, I began to wonder what his life's like now. Whether he tells the same old jokes, thinks the same old things, still talks incessantly about cars."

"In other words, if he were only more like us." She hands him her glass.

"Is that what I said?" he asks, pouring wine.

"Sounded that way to me."

"Shit!"

"What?"

"I've caught it, then. Klein flu. If you hang around the family long enough it happens."

"To everyone?"

"Eventually. And as far as I know, there isn't a cure."

"Oh, but I think you're better already," she says, rolling toward him, "just realizing you have it." And she pulls him down beside her, there on that last vestigial hill before the plains stretch as far as the eye can see to the west, baking amongst bluestem, rocks and cow chips, and they rest.

He rouses a half hour later, tossing off a heat shiver. And a dream.

He and Ronnie Blue were singing. A concert with a big crowd. Fireworks at the end. Their last number was to be the national anthem. A sing-along, everybody joining in. It was great. Big time. Bigger than they'd ever done. But when they came to the finale, it all fell apart. The music was off; and the words, although they seemed right, came out gibberish. The crowd laughed, then hooted, then started booing. Ronnie Blue dropped a match behind him. The whole place exploded as they finished their song.

Linda's awake. Of course. She wouldn't have slept. Not since he has a three-thirty meeting with George Murphy. A final rehearsal for the fireworks.

She has the picnic basket packed and is ready to go.

He hums. It sounds all right. She smiles.

He sings the first line. She asks why the sudden burst of patriotism.

A hawk descends in a gyre. It perches on a telephone pole alongside a road passing between a pasture and a milo field.

He isn't surprised in the least to see Ronnie Blue's car approaching.

Linda is. "What a strange coincidence."

They load their car and leave, meeting Ronnie Blue's convertible half way along the trail to the precipice. The black Thunderbird and silver Chevy stop side by side.

Ronnie Blue and his woman sit in the sun with the top down, hats shading their faces. The woman's—the girl's—eyes are emotionless. Bored. Ready to be elsewhere. She blinks at the wind.

And Ronnie Blue's grey, shiny washer eyes have gone red. Painful red. Painted red. Like eyes he's going to take out in a minute and laugh and say gotcha.

John Klein presses a button. His window lowers. "You old son of a gun. How are you, anyway?"

But Ronnie Blue only smiles. A line that crosses his mouth like ice cracking.

15

God, Ronnie!"

"You going to do nothing but bitch, or what? Should've left you with your mother."

"You told me you was going to show me a good time. The time of my life, you said."

"So?"

"Well, you ain't even half close. Not the way you acted back there."

"Just a joke, for christ's sake." He pitches a stone over the precipice. It skips and clatters to the field below. "Nobody can take a joke around here."

"That ain't the kind of thing you joke about."

"What a bunch of pussies."

"Nothing pussy about robbing banks."

"Nobody's robbed one yet, have they?"

"But you said—"

"Nobody's done anything. Have they?"

"Ain't nobody going to, either. Are they, Ronnie?"

"Will you just lay off."

"What if he tells somebody?"

"What if he does?"

"Couldn't they arrest us or something?"

"For what? Listen, him and me used to do a hell of a lot worse than that. He ain't going to tell nobody."

She locks her arms around her knees. "Let's go home, Ronnie. This ain't fun anymore. Let's just go home."

"We ain't done yet. Still got the fireworks and—"

"If you want me, take me home. You can have me soon as we get there. All you want."

"I can have you now, too. All I want."

He shoves her back, forcing her knees apart, pinning her shoulders to the rock. And he holds her there, wind catching in her pubic hair, sun drying her skin. He loves the smell. It drives him crazy. He wants to kiss her, make her close her legs on his head the way she does sometimes. Make her suck air and squirm. But he's not about to give her the satisfaction the way she's acting.

He gets up. She springs back into shape and rolls to her side.

"All I want. Any time I want."

"Take me home."

"We're staying."

"Take me to the highway. I'll hitch. I want to go home."

"What the hell's with everybody, treating me like I got some kind of disease or something. I have feelings, too, you know."

"So do I. And I ain't a dishrag. I ain't some goddamn old whore you can do whatever you want to."

"You're all I've got left."

"You've got yourself."

"But I need you."

"Right."

"I do. I need you to hold on to so I won't be like one of them balloons that gets loose and floats away. You know, floats on up there till you can't see it no more?" hand gesturing toward the sky.

"You are so full of shit."

The same hand draws back. She flinches. He turns away.

"Let's go get a drink."

She shrugs.

"When I say something I expect you to do more than just fucking sit there."

She gets up slowly. They shuffle to the car, dust puffing around their feet, bodies bent into the wind and blowing grit. The top of the hill has been scoured of all but a few tufts of grass, the earth eroded to hard clay and stone between them. Cattle trails, troughs gouged in the flinty soil, lead down from the hill on all sides. To and from food and water, over the same range buffalo once roamed. The buffalo were killed off, and the cattle come and go according to the price of beef. If they were cattle and someone saw them now, he wonders if they would be culled out and butchered while they still had some value. Before they died on the hoof.

"Come on," he says, grabbing her arm. "Snap to it, let's go. Hell of a birthday party this is."

In the car, she fishes under her seat for the Southern Comfort.

"It's the heat," he says. "Bakes your brain. Bakes you inside, too, till you don't want to do nothing. So chug-a-lug."

She shakes her head.

"I'm taking over the party. I'm making the party now. Drink!"

She sips.

"Tip the son of a bitch up!"

She gags, pulls her face away. Whiskey runs down her dress.

He gulps, bubbles riding up the glass bottle, shudders as he throws his head back, exhaling, imagining the fumes catching fire. A human blowtorch.

"How about something cold?" he says. "I want something cold."

She hands him seventy-five cents from her bag. "But that's it. That's all I've got left."

"You mean—"

"It's gone. Everything you told me to keep."

"Goddamn gypsies."

"Makes no difference how. It's still gone."

He stares along the trail down the hill, to the main road, to the horizon where dust fuses earth and sky. "Well, then."

She glances at him. Wary.

"What? What's that look about? This is Ronnie Blue, remember? And this here's my place. What I say goes. So you name it and you've got it. Hey-hey, whaddaya say? What's your pleasure?"

She hangs her head.

He laughs, starting the car, and sings.

The wind tears at them on the way back to town.

Just below the Santa Fe tracks, the Co-op station sits at an angle on the corner of South and Cottonwood Streets, across from the feed mill and the main Co-op office. It's an old grey stucco building with four pumps in a line out front, the drive entering on one side from South Street and on the other from Cottonwood. The space from the pumps out to the corner is usually filled with parked pickups. Today it's empty. The station is closed, tire racks, oil racks, signs, tow truck all locked in the service bays.

He pulls around back out of sight between two storage tanks. He used to work at the station evenings and weekends, and when they closed up at night they always left one window open in the back for ventilation. A habit's a habit.

He crawls through it, using the shop vac as a foothold, skirts the grease rack and slips into the office. The place smells like oil and new rubber. He likes it. He likes the old glass countertop, so scratched from coins you can't read the jokes underneath anymore. He likes the neat displays of additives, oil, tires, fan belts, batteries and the hundreds of fuses and bulbs sorted into small yellow drawers. It's the way he'll keep his own shop when he gets it. Only his will be bigger. And cleaner. And with a different place to hide the key to the Coke machine.

He lifts it from the nail inside the bathroom door where it has hung ever since he can remember. He opens the machine, takes out a half dozen cold cans and checks the cash box. At least they were smart enough to empty it before they left, and there's only a couple of dollars in the register. Not enough to get your ass in a jam over. The Snickers and Milky Ways look good, though, and he takes a few. Maybe she's hungry and some candy'll help, he doesn't know.

Before leaving, he flips on the switch to the pump out back where the Co-op trucks and tractors gas up. He pulls over and fills his tank. But he doesn't go back to switch the pump off. A little calling card. A reminder that they shouldn't be too trusting.

They drive north then over the tracks into town, drinking the Co-op's Cokes, eating their candy bars, burning their gas.

"How about a sandwich?" he says.

"Why are you doing this?"

He concentrates on mixing Southern Comfort in his Coke. He finally has a nice buzz on. He wants to keep it on.

"Ronnie?"

It's nothing she would understand. How he used to steal Twinkies from old man Hodges' ice cream shop next to the high school. How the old fart loved him in spite of who he was, how he could have gone broke and still not have suspected him. Not Ronnie Blue. God, he could make a killing in this town. Maybe he will. Maybe when this is all over he'll come back and sell aluminum siding from a fake company. "Ronnie Blue here. Remember me? Chester Blue's boy?" And they'll smile and think how nice it is somebody with so much against him turned out so well after all, as they sign on the dotted line. Then there's always storm windows and doors. Insulation. Cookware.

"This is silly, Ronnie. Stupid. Let's go."

He parks in a grove of trees up the road behind Raleigh's Hi-way Grocery, a little one room, quick-shop type place.

"Baloney? Ham? Cheese? What do you want?"

"Nothing."

"But you have to have something. Everybody has to have something."

He gets his tire iron from the trunk. His shotgun is wrapped in a blue blanket along the base of the back seat. It's a nice little gun. A couple of inches off the barrels gives the shot pattern a perfect spread, makes it harder to miss at close range. Him and Zimmerman use it for coyotes and jack rabbits. He always keeps it in his trunk. You never can tell when Zimmerman's going to get some wild hair.

He carries the tire iron inside his pants along his right leg. But there's no need to. There's nobody around. They're all at the park or home getting ready to go to the park. Dewey Cole and all his horse dick cop buddies, too. Hell, he could walk right in the front door and nobody'd know the difference. He might even be able to sell a couple of sandwiches to some out of town folks come to spend the day in the country. Sandwiches and chips and pop. Beer, too. He'd give them whatever they wanted. *Give* it to them. Now that would be fun, seeing how they act when he says it's on the house. But he wouldn't be able to do that, really. That'd be the easiest way he can think of to get caught and would probably have the worst consequences. People understand stealing stuff for yourself, but not giving it away.

Don Raleigh should be up here hauling garbage away from his back door instead of fucking Lauren all morning. Rotten lettuce and oranges and melons and who knows what all. Dogs have been in it after meat scraps. Tipped over the barrel, shit scattered everywhere, stinking damn water all over the step.

Raleigh's a fool. Nothing but a padlock. A measly padlock he rips out with one twist of the tire iron. Nobody in this whole damn town does any more than push a button on their door at night. And some not even that. The ones who do lock the door leave the windows open. One person, he can't remember who, put in an alarm system once. It didn't work and they had to get somebody from Wichita and finally Kansas City out to fix it. It was okay for a week then broke again. They said to hell with it. Neighbors is neighbors, ain't they? Friends?

He wipes his feet on the mat inside the door and closes it after him. Then he sets about making sandwiches and filling grocery bags with chips and pickles and cookies and Spam and mustard and beer. Cold beer from the cooler which he pries open. He drinks one while he works, and wonders whether Lauren Raleigh ever found anybody besides Don to fuck. At one time, she wanted him, Ronnie Blue. She told him Don was out till ten every Tuesday and Thursday night, if he was interested. And he would have gone, for damn sure. She had the nicest ass and legs in town. But somebody told him she only had one tit. The other was cut off. That stopped him stone cold. There's always something, always some damn thing. He's glad she still has Don.

He flaps open a couple more bags and begins filling them. Canned goods, milk, cheese, eggs, yeast, fish. Fish? Christ, he doesn't even like fish. Bread, jelly, peanut butter, Ovaltine, olive oil. Bag after bag, moving up and down the stubby little rows putting in whatever he lays hands on. He can't stop. He can't say why. He doesn't want to. It's there. He puts it in.

Now Fran Raleigh, Lauren's daughter, was something else again. She had everything. But she wouldn't give him the time of day.

Beets, okra, sauerkraut, Vienna sausages, doughnuts.

Once, from the front fender of Zimmerman's Bronco, he gutted a coyote with one shot.

Pepper, flour, shortening, nuts, Cheerios, ice cream. Seventeen bags lined up by the back door.

No matter how good it seems, there's always something.

He drives around to collect the groceries. He stacks them in the back seat and the trunk, burying the shotgun. And that's good. That's very good for now. He puts the last bag on Charlene's lap.

"You're nuts," she says. "I'm getting out of here."

"Go ahead. But it won't do you much good, since everybody's already seen you with me. I get busted, you get busted. Might as well stay for the ride."

She shakes her head and slumps against the door.

She isn't very pretty. He's known that, he supposes, but hasn't wanted to think about it. She's been fun, she's been a good time and a good lay and it'll be sad when he tells her it's finished. But he'll have to sooner or later.

Fran Raleigh used to worry he might "have" something from living around all that junk and she just didn't want to take a chance. She might change her mind, though, when he comes back, opens his place, starts over again, fresh.

He drives the length of Cottonwood Street and part way back up Maple, depositing a bag of groceries at each corner. He leaves two at

Mrs. Gaul's. All he keeps are the beer bag and one with their sandwiches and stuff for later. He feels good. Almost relieved.

"Now when people're on their way home, they'll have something to take for supper. They won't have to worry about it."

She says nothing. It's just as well.

On the way up Main Street he sees John Klein's black Thunderbird parked in a carport beside a double-wide trailer house.

He drives on. To the highway, out to the Baitshop and back past Klein's. He stops a half block away under a shade tree on a side street.

"God, I'm hungry," he says, reaching into the sandwich bag.

"I thought we'd at least go back to the park. Why're we—" She turns in the direction he's staring. "Oh, no!"

"Ain't these great?" speaking through a bite of sandwich. "Not half bad, even if I do say so myself. You better eat now. Get your strength up."

"Ronnie—"

"I don't know, I guess it's sort of like that guy says—that famous guy, I don't remember his name—he says, if you want money, you have to go to where the money is."

"This is a joke now, ain't it, Ronnie? I mean, this really has got to be a joke."

Swigging beer, he sits back with one hand on the wheel, legs spread. "I suppose you could say it is in one way. But I don't think anybody's going to be laughing."

16

$\mathcal{T}$wilight. It's already dark in the trailer. In the bedroom with the shades down.

They've been napping. They usually do after sex. Linda is still asleep, and he curls against her back, closing his eyes, as if to capture in some more permanent way her warmth, the feel of her skin, the musky smell of the sheet.

Rousing, she moves dreamily, rhythmically toward him, away, toward him, away, the two of them joining in a long and lazy dance before she finally rolls to her back, bringing him over on top of her. The perfect fit. Then the steady even climb, the quickening pace, harder and harder as they near the top. He feels himself leaving himself again, but this time not to sleep.

"It must be late," she says eventually, neither of them bothering to look at the clock on the night stand. "I suppose we'd better get going, although I'd rather stay here with you."

He runs his finger over her cheek to her chin to her lips. "No need to rush. We still have some light left."

"But I thought—"

"George has things under control. He's been torchman for fifteen

years now and he can get along without me. I'm guessing he prefers it
that way, truth be known."

"Well, not me. I don't ever want to do without you."

"Say that again."

"I don't ever want to do without you."

He kisses her.

She sits up. "I'm going to take a shower."

He nuzzles the back of her neck.

She stands, turning to face him. He lays his head sideways against
her breasts and hugs her.

"That's enough now," she says. "Otherwise we're not going to have
time to eat before the fireworks."

"We can get something down there."

"I'd really rather fix supper here," she says. "If you don't mind too
much. We can throw a salad together and have some of that good
white Bordeaux we opened the other night. Why don't you work on
it while I'm in the bathroom, and I'll finish while you clean up."

He puts on his robe and goes to the kitchen. Lettuce, cucumber,
carrot, tomato. Peanuts. Black olives.

It's amazing what good sex can do for your mood, he thinks, wish-
ing they could back up part of the day and replay it—Mrs. Mayhew's,
take two; swimming pool, take two—with a new script, a new attitude. But what's done is done and right now they couldn't be feeling
much better about each other—or anything else, for that matter—at
least as far as he's concerned.

He dumps the slimy remains of a bag of bean sprouts into the
garbage disposal and piles the other things in the draining rack to peel
and wash.

Cheese.

He smiles, hums a tune he hasn't thought about in years.

The last deep purple shades of sunset ripple over Mrs. Black's living room windows across the street.

He turns on the light above the sink, switches it off again. Immediately, without thinking.

The bastard. The dumb bastard.

He steps quickly over to the living room, to the big windows, as if looking out from there will make a difference. He pulls the drape back slowly and peers around it.

A half block away, Ronnie Blue is sitting up on the back of the driver's seat of his parked car, what looks like a beer can in his hands as he leans, elbows on knees, toward the house. His woman, seemingly unchanged since they saw her at Miller's Hill, stares woodenly out the windshield of the car. They could be people waiting for a concert to begin. Or a race. A festival of some kind. Just waiting.

"John?"

He drops the drape.

"Jo-hn?"

She comes out of the bathroom, fluffing her damp hair with a towel. "I wanted to tell you we should probably get rid of the rest of those—are you all right?"

"Yeah, except I'm kind of tired. You wouldn't have any idea why that would be, would you?" he smiles.

"But you're all pale, like you're about to faint. Sit down."

Untying his robe, he wanders toward the bed. "I couldn't find any salad dressing."

"Don't worry about that. I can make some." Head and body swathed in towels, she sits beside him, holds his hand in hers. "What's wrong, John? What's going on?"

He glances at her, the hallway, back. "He's here."

"*Him?*"

A nod.

"Here?" cocking an ear toward the living room.

"No. Outside. Parked over by Chandlers'."

"Call the police," she says.

"I can't do that."

"*I* can."

"What will you say? Some guy's parked out on the street?"

"He threatened you, John."

"Not *me*."

"He said he was going to rob the bank."

"He said he *could*, Linda. Just could. There's a lot of difference."

"So what are you going to do, sit around and wait to see if he does? They can at least watch him, keep an eye on him."

"I suppose so, except you don't know the guy like I do. It's all vintage Blue. Even this. A lot of huffing and puffing and chest beating. And he's drunk to boot. Did you see his eyes?"

"All the more reason," she says.

"I don't know, it wouldn't seem right somehow."

"Right? What do you mean *right*?"

"I grew up with him. I know him. I've always been able to talk to him."

"John, please, you're not making sense."

"And so far he hasn't really done anything. That could be part of it, too, you know. The intimidation thing. Since he made the remark in the first place, he had to do something to keep from looking stupid in front of his woman. So he parks out there and has a good chuckle because he knows we're in here stewing around."

"But what if it turns into more than that, more than just a bluff?"

"I don't know."

"Then that's it. I'm calling right now."

The doorbell rings.

She freezes half way to the phone.

The bell rings again. An obnoxious bing-bong, not even on key.

"All right, damn it." He stands, yanking his robe together.

Tears fill her eyes.

"I have to talk to him, don't I? I owe him that much anyway. You said so yourself, remember?"

"But that was before—"

He holds her, kisses her forehead. "Everything's going to be all right. You'll see. It will be."

Before unlocking the front door, he straightens his robe, cinches the belt.

Ronnie Blue's eyes are clearer now. Shiny grey. Metallic. Pupils widening in the fading light, round and dark as the openings of the gun barrels showing under the edge of a blanket.

"If I were you, Ronnie, I'd—"

"If I were you, John, I'd just step right on back inside."

17

The door clicks shut behind him. A clean, solid sound, the bolt latching. He can see it for an instant snapping into place. The parts coming together as they should, as they were designed to.

Everything seems sharper now that he's here, as if this were the moment the whole day has been moving toward. The air so cold it hurts to breathe. The bead of sweat on John Klein's lip, the way he ties and reties the belt of his robe, backwards, fingers thinking through each loop and crossing like a kid learning to tie his shoelaces. The clock with no numbers on the kitchen wall. The smell of lettuce, rug shampoo, nerves, sex.

"Where is she?"

John Klein's hands pause, thumbs hooking in the belt.

"Miss Clean. Where the hell is she?"

"Home. She went to change clothes."

"No horseshit, Klein. I've been over there an hour and I—"

"She left the back way. Down the alley."

Ronnie Blue nods at the bedroom door.

"Open it."

"I told you—"

"Open it! You got nothing to hide, you got nothing to worry about."

Dressed now, she's sitting on the bed, head down, hands folded in her lap, like someone who's been told to be seated, the surgeon will see her soon.

"Well, well."

"Why didn't you hide?" John Klein says.

"From what?" Ronnie Blue moves around them, gun trained chest-high on Linda. "Ain't no reason to hide. She's too pretty for that anyway. Shouldn't keep something that pretty out of sight."

He wags the gun. She gets up.

"Yes, sir, I'd say you done mighty well for yourself, Mr. Klein. Smells pretty, too, just like I thought. Miss Clean, sure enough."

"Her name is Linda."

"Her name's whatever I want it to be."

She takes John Klein's arm, restraining him.

"That's right. You just pay attention to her and you'll be a lot better off. She understands. She knows who's calling the shots now."

They walk in front of him past the kitchen to the living room. She is nice. Thin. Good legs, a smile forming where they join her hips. Straight back. A soft, gentle swell from waist to shoulders. It's really too bad he won't have time to get to know her better.

"Now why don't you folks just sit down there on the couch and relax. We all need to relax. In fact, it looks like I busted in here right at suppertime. I already ate myself, but if you want to go ahead—"

"Nobody's hungry," John Klein says.

"Suit yourself. But if I was you, I'd have something. Never know what'll come up before you get your next bite."

"Meaning?" John Klein leans forward.

"Nothing. Just saying I'd eat's all. As for myself, I'd like a cold beer, if you have one."

Linda stands.

"Whoa!" Too fast. Too goddamn fast. The gun pointing midway between her throat and cleavage before he knows it. Before he even realizes he's done it. "Now. Sit back down and get up again. Slow. I don't like jumping around. That's when accidents happen, and I don't want no accidents." He lowers the gun with her. "You see, this here gun's got what's called a hair trigger. Now, that means—"

"You don't have to explain," she says.

"What that means," he goes on, voice dropping for more dramatic emphasis, "is this trigger's set so fine all I need's a couple of ounces of pressure to pull it. Like a twitch, maybe. A nervous twitch."

"How convenient," she says.

"If you mean I don't miss a whole lot with it, you're right. John here'd know that. Him and me puffed up a few quail and pheasants and one or two coyotes in our time. Ain't that right, John?"

"One or two."

"You do any hunting now?"

"Not much."

"What you do do's probably on them—what do you call them?— 'hunting parties' where you and the big boys all get together for a trip up to the Dakotas or Idaho, Montana, something like that."

"No, I've never—"

"I heard about one of them once. Bunch of guys out in Missouri the first day of deer season. Killed ten head of cattle before they was finished. You ever heard tell of such as that? Having all that brain power and still not knowing a goddamn cow from a deer."

They both stare back at him, deadpan.

"Well, you ought to know what the hell you're shooting at, hadn't you? Sure, you should. Now how about that beer? You was on your way to see if there wasn't one over there, ain't that right, Miss Clean? And while you're at it, bring one for my friend here."

John Klein shakes his head.

"Let's not have any of that shit. I never knew you when you wasn't thirsty. And you've got to be thirstier than ever right now. Ain't that so? Besides, I don't like to drink alone. It ain't healthy. Especially when you're celebrating."

She brings two Coors.

"What about you?"

"I don't like beer."

"That's right, beer's for women, wine's for ladies. Ain't that how it goes? Well, get yourself some wine, then. And not just any old junk, either. Something special."

She holds out the Bordeaux.

"Looks fancy enough to me. 'Course I wouldn't know. Now pour it and get on back over here with us. I want to make a toast."

She sits again beside John Klein.

Ronnie Blue raises his beer can. "To the birthday boy. Me. Drink up."

"Cheers."

"Many happy returns."

"Bet you didn't even remember, did you? Bet you forgot, sure as hell. Ronnie Blue and the good old U. S. of A., too? Yes, sir. The last time we had us a celebration was—why, it must've been five years ago. You and me and the Whitman girls. Remember now? Hell, we was all over the place that night, and they was all over us. Just having a hell of a time. And you sang. Out at Watkins' Dam. By god if you didn't. Sing now."

"I don't feel like it."

"That's too bad. Fetch him another beer, Miss Clean. Maybe that'll loosen things up. Lubricate the old vocal cords."

"I don't want another beer. I don't want to sing."

"Stubborn as ever. How do you stand being around somebody this stubborn?"

"I haven't had the problem," she says.

"Go on, sing. I'm waiting."

"No," John Klein says.

"I was good enough for you once. Sing."

"Stick it up your ass."

He stands, the gun aimed between John Klein's eyes.

"Sing!"

"Happy birthday to you," Linda begins, shaky at first, then with more control. "Happy birthday to you. Happy birthday, dear—What do you want me to call you?"

"My name'll be fine."

"Happy birthday, dear Ronnie, happy birthday to you."

"There. See there? You could've done that. Why didn't you?"

"You've made your point," John Klein says. "You can go now."

"Oh, but I ain't even started yet. Christ, no. I ain't even started."

"What you've done so far is bad enough, Ronnie. But you still have a chance to walk away."

"Whoa, now. Looks to me like you're forgetting who's in charge here."

"I'm only telling you for your own good."

"Like you always did? Big Papa. Big Brother. Do this and that. This and that. But not that. And look at you now. Who're you telling me to do anything? What makes you such hot shit? Your car? Your woman? Your house? I got all that, man. The only thing I ain't got's money, and I'll have it soon enough."

"I have a few dollars. Fifty or seventy-five. You can have that. You can have that and still walk out of here, no questions asked. But that's as far as I can go, Ronnie."

"Chicken feed. Petty cash. I'm talking big bucks here, not your pocket change, Mr. Banker. Mr. Bigshot Banker. I want it all."

"Don't you see how stupid you're being?"

"Save the speeches."

"You're looking at a lot of years, Ronnie. Thirty at least."

"Got no choice."

"Sure you have."

"Can it!" Ronnie Blue jumps up, throat dry, fingers dancing on the gun stock. He pulls the curtain back. Charlene is still in the front seat. Like a statue. Like a mannequin he'll have to move the arms and legs of to get it in and out of the car. "I've got no time for that crap. You understand? I'm doing what I'm doing and that's it. Hell, who knows? I might even turn out to be a hero. Like that Cooper guy that stole all that money and jumped out of the airplane and they never did find him? Remember that? People'll probably tell stories about me, write songs. Make movies. Someday you can bounce your grand-kids on your knee and say you knew that Blue. He was a friend of yours. Once. You can tell them you was there the day he robbed the bank. You was the one who opened the vault and filled all them bags while he stood there watching, saying more, more, like he couldn't ever get enough. And they'll love that. They'll love you and they'll love me for doing it. And you can say the last time you heard, Ronnie Blue was making it big in Brazil."

"That's a nice story, but—"

"No time for buts. No time for any more talking."

"But—You'll have to excuse me, I don't know how else to say it. Because time is all we have."

"What the hell're you—"

John Klein hunches his shoulders. "There's a time lock on the vault."

"Yeah? So?"

"I can't open it."

"Bullshit!"

"I can't. Nobody can. It'll open automatically at seven-thirty in the morning. And there's no way to override it."

"Come on."

"No way."

"You're feeding me a line." His neck aches, the backs of his legs. "He's feeding me a line, ain't he?"

"No," Linda says. "They installed it two years ago. I remember the day because he took me down and showed me."

"Get your old man over here."

"What good's—"

"Because I got no reason at all to believe either one of you. Now, do I? Call him."

John Klein glances at Linda. She nods.

He watches Klein go to the phone. He walks like a duck. Feet out. They'd flap if they weren't on the rug. There's always something. There's always some goddamn thing. And the hair on his calves has been rubbed off. Bald spots like the one on the back of his head. People don't even look like they should.

"Turn around. I want to see you. I want to hear you."

He's holding the receiver in both hands, like he's afraid he'll drop it.

"Dad? Glad I caught you before you left. No, not yet. Listen, I—"

Ronnie Blue swings the gun around.

"Do you think you could come by the house for a minute? No, right away. And by yourself. I need to talk to you. Yes, it's that serious. All right. See you."

They sit. He paces. They wonder what he's going to do, and so does he.

Time. Fucking time.

A car drives up. A big car. Maybe a Buick?

He hides just inside the bedroom door, Linda with him, enough of the gun sticking out to show he means business.

Side by side, Bud and John Klein are hard to tell apart. Bud Klein's thicker, balder, but not by much. In a few years they'll look like twins.

He wonders if things would have been different had he looked more like his old man.

Bud Klein squints at the bedroom door. Seeing the gun, he shakes his head, turns to talk with his son.

"None of that shit," Ronnie Blue says, disguising his voice with his hand. "Over here. I want to know everything you say."

John Klein tells what's happened, like he's reciting an outline or something. A report. Just the facts. Nothing but the facts.

Bud Klein comes toward the door then, head thrust forward like somebody about to talk to a camera.

Ronnie Blue exposes a few more inches of the gun.

Bud Klein stops, arms out.

"Look, whoever you are, what John says is true. There is a time lock that can't be overridden, except by a technician from Wichita. Here, see?" He holds up a printed card from the American Lock Company. A name. A couple of phone numbers. "Now we could call them, but I don't think that would help you much. It'd be a whole lot like ringing an alarm, and I'm sure that's not what you have in mind. So—"

Ronnie Blue wiggles the gun.

Bud Klein steps back. "What's that mean?"

"I think he wants you to shut up," John Klein says.

"But this is silly. This is absurd." Bud Klein's feet stutter as he turns from his son to the gun and back. "Where's Linda?"

"In there. With him."

"But—"

"It's okay."

"But I don't see—How about your own money? Your mother and I have some, too."

"I tried."

"And there are some other things. Jewelry and such."

"He wants the vault opened."

"But he can't have that. Doesn't he understand? That's the one thing he can't have."

"I told him. He wanted to hear it from you."

"All right, I said it. Now what?"

"I don't know."

"Well, he can't stay here forever."

"I think he realizes that, Dad."

"Sooner or later—"

"Dad!"

Bud Klein peers impatiently at his son, then, suddenly paling, glances up and around, as though he has heard a voice, seen a vision. He bolts toward the door, out of his son's reach, drawing up with the barrels just inches from his face.

Ronnie Blue can smell the nervous sweat, the lime aftershave, gun oil.

"You can't! Do you hear me, whoever the hell you are? You can't do this!"

Spit sprays through the crack in the door onto Ronnie Blue's hands. He smiles.

"There are consequences! There will be consequences!"

Bud Klein sinks back. Spent. Stooped. Hands to his face. Maybe he's crying. That'd be a hell of a note, Bud Klein crying. What would he be crying for?

John Klein steps forward. "Is it all right if he, you know, goes now?"

Two people're bad enough. Three would be a mess. He jerks the gun barrels toward the door.

"But I can't leave you—and her—here," Bud Klein says. "Not with the likes of him."

"You've done everything you can. Go on. Be with Mom."

"Oh, damn! Your mother. What am I going to tell her?"

"What's happened. The truth."

Bud Klein grips his son's shoulder, hugs him.

"We'll be okay," John Klein says. "Listen to me now. We'll be all right. Trust me."

At the front door, Bud Klein wheels around, finger out. "You'll pay for this! Mark my words. There's a price, and you'll pay!"

The motor of the big car roars. Tires squeak on the drive. A rocker panel scrapes the curb. Rubber burns.

"What an old fuzzball," Ronnie Blue says, throwing the door open. "Now I'd guess we've got about two minutes to disappear. So let's get hopping."

John Klein starts to the bedroom.

"Wrong way."

"My clothes."

"Only thing you'll need's your car keys."

"Car keys?"

"I figure if we're going out, we might as well go out in style. Don't you think?"

18

$\mathcal{I}$t's the gun, John Klein thinks. That's what makes the difference.

He drives his Thunderbird into the Kansas dusk, stubble fields and hedgerows and the darkening sky as familiar as the clap of gravel under the car, west toward last light and the great expanding plain, over the familiar roads of their youth. Here they drank, here they laughed, here they argued, here they pawed desperately at girls who wanted to but couldn't say yes.

Then there was no gun.

There was no bank.

There was no money.

It was a charmed time. A single blazing year which, like certain comets, passes, never to be witnessed again.

In the mirror he sees Ronnie's and Linda's heads in the back seat, shotgun upright between them, silhouetted against a dust screen luminous in the lights of Ronnie Blue's Chevy Charlene is driving behind them. A movie through a peephole. A movie with no music, no words, no movements, save those generated by the road. A movie with no faces, reversing toward its end.

Then there was no time lock.

"Stop," Ronnie Blue says.

The ditch is filled with weeds, bottles and cans, paper leached to pulp. Dust settling through the headlights like mist.

"Get out. Not you. Her."

Linda folds the seat forward and reaches for the handle.

John Klein touches her arm, her shoulder.

She falls on him, clinging with all her strength.

"Go on," he tells her. "Do as he says. I'll be all right."

"But—" her eyes frozen in the lights of Ronnie Blue's car.

"There's nothing to be afraid of."

She stands beside the road, hand raised in a tentative goodbye.

"I love you," he says.

As they leave, the Chevy's headlights catch her, hold her a moment, then release her to the night. He wonders when he'll see her again.

At the next intersection, Ronnie Blue waves the gun. "Turn north."

Behind them, the fireworks are beginning. Streaks of light bursting, blooming, booming.

"Happy birthday," John Klein says.

"Now east."

Behind them, Ronnie Blue's car misses the turn, shoots a hundred yards up the road, slows, surges on.

"Where the fuck is she going?"

The southern sky sparkles and crackles, alive with color. He can almost hear the oohs and aahs, the anxious tittering of children.

"Pull over by the tracks."

It hasn't occurred to him until now that there are three of them in two cars. It doesn't make sense. Doesn't seem right.

"Get out."

"If it's my car you want, go ahead and take it."

"Out!"

"Or pitch the keys over into that field or something."

The Chevy hasn't appeared yet. Ronnie Blue fidgets like somebody who needs to go to the bathroom.

"Start walking. Toward the bridge."

"With no shoes? What are you, nuts? I won't have any feet left by the time I get down there."

"Walk, goddamn it, this ain't no picnic."

"Come on, man. I've got tennies in the back."

"All right, if it'll speed your ass up."

The trunk light floods their feet, grey with dust. He unzips the satchel, takes out his shoes. He only bought them a month ago, but the toes are already scuffed, one ankle pad fraying. Used to be it made a difference what you paid for things.

"Get them on. Hurry up."

The sky sizzles and whistles and pops, catching fire, fading.

"What do you think of that?" John Klein says, lifting his head in the direction of the fireworks. "All in your honor, too."

"Cut the chit-chat."

He slams the trunk lid. "What do you expect? You want me just to lie down? Kiss your feet? Kiss your ass? I don't plan on making this any easier for you than I have to."

"Move."

"Yes, sir."

"And I'll take the robe now."

"Yes, sir. Whatever you say, sir."

His skin is ashen, prickly. It's not his skin. The tracks, black and white stripes between them, leading off into the night aren't like any place he's ever been.

"How far, sir?"

Ronnie Blue gazes at John Klein's tennis shoes, his underpants, his bare chest, as if not quite believing what he sees, but having to because of the gun, its two dark holes punctuating their every word, their every move.

19

He has to be fucking crazy, that's all.

John Klein moves slowly in front of him, like someone walking underwater, every other step his shoe striking the ballast between ties. Tap-crunch, tap-crunch, tap-crunch, the shotgun aimed at his back marking cadence.

Nothing else explains it. What he's doing here. Why he ever came back in the first place.

Where is she? Charlene.

John Klein stops, turns. "This far enough?"

"Keep moving," gun trained kidney-high.

Crunch-crunch, crunch-tap, crunch. Tap-crunch, tap-crunch, as he regains stride.

Stealing pop and groceries is one thing. But not this, for Christ's sake. Not kidnapping and robbery. *Attempted* robbery, at that. Not a goddamn cent. And now Klein and that woman of his.

Fucking fireworks.

Where is Charlene?

Somebody's nervous. Real nervous, the piss smell Carl had that day going right through everything—the heat and dust, itch weed and creosote. But he can't tell for sure where it's coming from. Him or Klein.

"Now?"

"Shut up and keep walking."

"I'm tired. It doesn't make any difference where you do it, does it? Here or farther on?"

"Do what?"

"Kill me."

"Who said anything about killing? Now march."

Maybe he should have let Klein put his clothes on like he wanted to. There's something pitiful, sad, about a grown man out at night in nothing but his underpants and shoes.

"Just one favor," he says. "Leave Linda alone."

But that's what cowboys used to do, take people's clothes. Better than taking their guns or anything.

"She's got nothing to do with any of this. She's innocent."

And that's what he's planning to do. Leave him down at the first bridge, shoes off. Just leave him, so there'll be time to make a getaway.

The sky glows and darkens, like there's some big neon sign out there he wishes the hell he could unplug. And all that booming and cracking and whizzing he can do without, too.

Where is she?

Just leave him.

Maybe tie him.

"In a way, I'm almost sorry this didn't work out," John Klein is saying. "The robbery, that is. At least then you'd have had some money for your efforts and you could have ended up in the history books right there with the rest of them. I mean, hell, you might even have—"

And gag him.

Where *is* that woman?

No shoes. Take his underpants. Naked and barefoot and tied up, he won't go anywhere for a while.

A car swings parallel to the tracks. He glances over his shoulder. The lights click to high beams.

Pain whitens his sight. Like looking into a blast furnace, his old man's face shiny from shaving.

The shotgun tugs in his hands. Dipping to his right, he swings up and forward, gun butt first.

John Klein goes to his hands and knees, teeth scattered on ties like white flower petals.

She's running, gasping.

"Ronnie! Ronnie!"

Klein spits blood, growls.

Boy! Get him boy! his old man shouts.

Klein lunges.

Mad dog!

The gun bucks. Klein drops, rolling to his back, arms and legs stirring the air.

"Jesus, Ronnie! Oh, no!"

"He grabbed it. Now get back."

"But you're not going to—"

"Wouldn't leave an animal like this. Go on! Move it!"

Hand to her mouth, she turns and runs toward the lights.

For his own good, boy. It's for his own good.

He places the barrels behind John Klein's ear, looks away and fires.

Poor bastard.

The body slides over the embankment. A soft roll into the weeds.

Straightening, he peers along the tracks. A half mile down, a signal light is green. He wonders if he should take that as a sign. But he doesn't believe in signs. Never has.

20

*C*old. All the windows up and the heater on, he's so cold.

"Don't lose me this time," he told her.

John Klein's car blasts down the dark tunnel between hedgerows.

"Don't lose me."

Sweating and he's still cold. Shivering, dry-throated cold. If he talked, he'd squeak.

She hasn't lost him, either. This time she's staying with him.

If he could just keep that face out of his mind. But it's every place he looks. On the inside of the wind-shield. On the speedometer. Blurring across the dash.

JOHN KLEIN

You get your name engraved, inset on a little plaque above the radio, if you buy a limited edition car.

JOHN KLEIN

You get your name engraved on a tombstone if you're dead.

When will they find him and what will they do?

How?

His woman.

But he promised. Or almost promised. She had nothing to do with it.

Charlene fishtails behind him. Like kids tearing down the road doing wheelies on their bikes.

If she doesn't tell, somebody else will. What difference does it make who?

One thing for goddamn sure, he's not going to go peacefully. Not Ronnie Blue. He'll outrun and outshoot them down to the last man.

That might even be good enough for the national news.

JOHN KLEIN

Ronnie Blue.

He never knew you could be so cold in the summertime.

The highway's smooth as deep, dark water. So quiet and even he can't feel the road, can't hear it except for the splat of tires on tar strips.

That face. Klein. His old man. Klein.

He presses the heels of his hands to his eyes.

Seventy-five going on eighty.

She's still there.

He slows, sets the cruise control on fifty-five. Cruise control? Jesus, had things gotten that bad? But it's good for now. He can't afford any more fuck-ups. He has to think.

He wishes he had a cigarette and he doesn't even smoke. He wishes he had something.

A drink. But it's all in the other car.

Think. He needs to think. Plan ahead.

The lights of Newton glow above the trees at the next curve. God, have they come that far? He doesn't even remember Walton. The park. The restaurant where the patrol car hides out of sight on the south side. He has to be more careful.

Use his head.

Why'd he do it? Why couldn't he have just left well enough alone? Always grabbing. Always trying to run things.

JOHN KLEIN

Get your name engraved on the dashboard. See your name while you're driving. Remind you who you are.

Probably one just like it on his desk at the bank.

JOHN KLEIN

And at home?

Maybe she has one, too, his woman, where she lives.

A name instead of a face.

He reaches toward the radio, draws back. He's not sure what's going to happen the first time he hears "Ronnie Blue." And he'll see himself, too, on television, in newspapers.

Ronnie Blue, how do you do?

If he'd have just kept his hands off. For once.

He starts up the ramp to the Newton by-pass. Beautiful downtown Newton. Wards. Penney's. A half dozen flower shops. God only knows why so many. A couple of drugstores, a hardware or two. Hospitals and the Santa Fe depot where you can catch the 2:35 a.m. for L.A.

The cruise control moves the accelerator under his foot. Hell, he doesn't have to do anything. He could just set the car on automatic pilot and get out and walk.

Charlene's signaling, flashing her lights for him to pull over.

It's too open here, too conspicuous. In town's no good, either. They know Klein's car. They remember his. What the hell is she thinking?

He hits the brake pedal.

Still she signals.

Dumb—

Tires squeal as he swerves at the last instant to catch the Broadway exit.

"What?" he says, running back to his car. "What do you want?"

Her arms are locked against the wheel, hair a tangle from the wind, her new hat mashed in the back seat.

"Where are we going?" she says.

"Back. Home."

"They'll find you. Us."

"Not if we're smart. Not for a while."

"You killed him."

"Just follow me. Don't lose me."

"Goddamn, Ronnie. Goddamn."

He gets back in and swings over to the entrance ramp.

She hesitates, head turning with Klein's car, then slowly, as if drugged and reviewing to herself each movement, comes around into line.

There's a cop at the rest stop seven miles on. Taking a piss. Looking for queers. Looking for junkies.

Fifty-five.

He wonders if they've found him yet, what'll happen when they do.

The cop stands by his car. No hat, short sleeves, gun snug as a growth on his hip.

Charlene honks as they pass by.

The cop waves. Feeling good. Feeling important. Blondes belong in convertibles. Traveling alone. No underpants.

What would she say if he pulled her over? What would she do?

Damn you, John Klein.

The cop gets into his cruiser, pulls past a parked semi and onto the ramp.

Fifty-five.

He comes down, even with them. Big nose, moustache, skin so white it looks like a mask.

Halloween. Trick or treat. All kinds of goodies when you're dressed like a cop. People telling you how great it'd be if you grew up and became a *real* policeman. Fireman. Teacher. Preacher. Butcher, baker, candlestick maker. Banker. Anything but a junkman. Even a clown or a bum's better than that. People at least laugh at them.

The cop merges behind Charlene. Big nose. Big dick. Horse dick he can take off and lay on the seat beside him. Maybe that's what she's been wanting. Horse cock.

What would she say?

God *damn* you, John Klein. Couldn't keep your hands off.

Should have brought her along. His woman. What's her name— Linda? For a couple of days. To look at. To get to know better.

She's walking into somebody's house right now. Yard light bleaching everything. Bones left out in the sun. Big fucking dog making enough racket to raise the—

Can I use your phone? There's been a—

JOHN KLEIN

Just a couple of days. Long enough to figure things out.

She'd understand. With time, she'd come to understand what happened.

The cop peels off at the Valley Center exit. Checking in? Going home to lie next to his wife and wonder about the blonde in the Chevy convertible?

Have coffee?

If she'd give him a chance, he could explain.

But a promise is a promise. And he kept it.

And that's something.

That's something, John Klein.

Just past the 235 turn-off, down 135 into Wichita. The light tunnel. His heart pounds. His stomach rises. Butter light, false sunlight that washes out color and distance, place and time, and hurls him along like something fired from a cannon, blasted into yellow space, deeper and deeper into it, out of himself, faster and faster, until he wants to scream.

Eighty-five.

Ninety-five.

JOHN KLEIN

He comes out the other side. Braking. A deep breath.

Twenty-first Street.

He wonders for a moment where he's been. But he knows now, strangely, where he's going. As if he's known from the very beginning.

Is that what people will think? Later, when they've broken it down and are trying to fix it? Trying to figure out the why's and where's? The how's.

Maybe they'll take his brain and put it in a jar. Stand and stare at it. Study it, hands behind them, stooping to see better. Going around and around.

And he'll look back from his mind's eye.

Smiling.

Ronnie Blue, how do you do?

Shaking their confidence.

They'll miss John Klein.

They'll remember Ronnie Blue.

Just like he said.

She's still there. Right behind him. Down the Central Avenue ramp. Over to Hydraulic. To Douglas. The *Eagle-Beacon* parking lot, where he pulls in like he belongs.

She waits at the curb, lights off. With him now. The way it used to be with sex. When they still cared what was good and what wasn't. What helped and what didn't.

There's an opening next to the editor's reserved space. Black Thunderbirds don't need an introduction.

JOHN KLEIN

He smiles.

With his pocketknife, he digs the nameplate out of the dash and carries it with him to the gate, dropping it in the trash on his way out.

21

*C*hicken heads. Combs, beady eyes, pointy beaks wobbling by like old people paying their last respects. Clucking, gurgling past. The sound of water in a sluggish drain.

They circle him. Some perch on the rim of his casket.

But *he* isn't dead. He just can't move, can't talk.

A hen nests by his right ear and lays an egg. A rooster crows above his head.

They flock in, feeding.

Pecking. Gouging. Tearing skin.

Senses back, he sits up and clambers out, chickens flapping, squawking, regrouping behind him.

Dogs now, snapping at his heels as he climbs. Coyotes. Frothing. One red-mouthed bitch with guts trailing.

He lifts a boulder and hurls it at them.

John Klein. His body wheeling spread-eagle into black space.

He loses his balance and falls. A net catches him. He bounces up, up toward a figure peering from a circle of light.

Zimmerman.

Scraggly black hair. A three-day growth of beard. Cigarette.

Watery eyes. A red tank top over a beer belly that nearly touches his thighs when he sits. His old man told him once about a guy in Germany whose stomach was so big he had to push it around in a wheelbarrow. Zimmerman in ten years.

But Zimmerman doesn't give a shit, and that's why he likes him. He doesn't know anything Zimmerman cares about, except maybe him, Ronnie Blue. And him maybe even more than himself. Isn't Zimmerman the only one in this whole goddamn day who wished him happy birthday? Without being asked. Just did it because he remembered and felt the hell like it. That's Zimmerman.

"What're you doing here, man?"

It is Zimmerman's bedroom. Clothes overflowing a cardboard box in one corner, a motorcycle against the wall in the other. Willie Nelson and Waylon Jennings posters taped to the closet door. Holes in the ceiling where he tried to put a mirror above the bed. The air stinking of grease and stale smoke.

"I needed a place to hole up."

"Could've told me. Could've said something, for Christ's sake. Come home and my goddamn window's broke out. Why, hell, I thought there's burglars in here. You're just lucky, that's all. Lucky as hell I saw your car in the garage first."

"Where you been?"

"Working."

"On the Fourth?"

"A place out by the airport—a motor pool. They needed somebody pronto. A friend of Cal's works there. Cal told him about me. The guy called around noon and I went. Started right in. Nobody's fucked me over yet, so I may stay."

"Then I guess I couldn't have told you, could I? Even if I'd wanted to."

"Guess not." Zimmerman pinches the last half inch of cigarette into a saucer on the night stand and throws the filter into a wastebasket. "You really do it? You really waste that dude?"

"Yeah."

"Jesus!"

"It was an accident."

"That ain't what they're saying."

"Well, that's what it was. When did they find him?"

"Didn't hear. Most of it's about kidnapping and murder. Heavy stuff, man. And trying to rob a goddamn bank. What the hell'd you do that for?"

"Money."

"Shit, dumb as I am, I wouldn't even try that. Why not a liquor store or a filling station?"

"Where's Charlene?"

"Sleeping on the couch when I came in."

"The couch?"

"Yeah, I didn't even know it was her there for a minute, she looks so strung out."

He nods. "It's been rough on her."

Zimmerman lights another cigarette, cupping the match to his face and peering over his hands like a cowboy keeping an eye on the herd.

"So what're you planning now?" he says, flipping out the match.

"Don't know yet."

"When do you think you will?"

"When I figure it out."

"My ass is grass if they know you've been here." He taps the cigarette, ash dropping six inches short of the saucer. "So I was thinking—"

"Save it."

"I was thinking the sooner you move on—"

"Where, Zimmerman? Just goddamn it tell me where."

"I know, man, but— I mean, I can get twenty years just for talking to you."

"'Anytime.' Remember that? 'Anytime I needed anything, all I had to do was—"

Zimmerman slams his fist onto the night stand. "That don't include shooting people in the fucking head. Never did. I mean, Jesus, man, in the head. Blew it away. That ain't normal. That ain't 'anytime.'"

"You want to hear what really happened?"

Zimmerman hitches his butt around like he's got saddle sores. His cowboy walk. Straight toward Waylon and Willie, away from Ronnie Blue. He talks to them.

"I can make out a couple of days. Go over to my brother Ed's, tell him I'm having my place exterminated or something. He'll get a kick out of that. You remember Ed, he'll know I'm up to my ass in something. Probably think some old boy's after me for having his woman, that sort of thing. But he don't like me around his kids too long. Thinks I'm a bad influence or something. I can see his point." He half turns, one eye on the bed. "After that, though—"

"Yeah, yeah."

"But the place is yours till then. I don't mind. Really, I don't. But I would appreciate it if—"

"Don't worry. Nobody'll know we're here."

"Especially Gus," Zimmerman says. "He watches the place like he owns it."

"We'll be careful."

"Well—"

"Will you just go on?"

Zimmerman mashes the cigarette in the saucer. "Got to pick up a few things first. Jeans and stuff for work, you know. And—oh, yeah, there's a bunch of food in the refrigerator. I went out yesterday and—"

"Okay, thanks."

"Listen, man, I—" a pained expression, hand out. "I mean, I really wish—" The hand drops.

Ronnie Blue rolls over, staring at the motorcycle, listening to the drawers opening and shutting, Zimmerman's and Charlene's voices in the living room, the door latching, Zimmerman's car backing out and driving off quieter than he's ever heard.

He closes his eyes, pulls his knees up to his chest, folds his arms over the top of his head and squeezes. Squeezes until he can't hear or feel a thing.

He wonders where they got the picture. From his mother, he supposes. Or the school. It's an old one. He looks like a kid with that stringy hair and dippy smile.

It's not right. If they're going to show him around all over the place, they ought to use a picture that does him justice. Like the one he's got at home, the one he had taken at a studio a couple of months ago. A present for Charlene. She didn't have a picture of him of any kind, and she wanted one. A nice one, a portrait. Maybe he should ask her if he could send it in to the TV station.

That might at least give them something to talk about. She hasn't said more than a half dozen words since they've been at Zimmerman's. Last night she slept. He can understand that. And part of this morning, too. Catching up. But this afternoon? And now again tonight? God, you'd think she'd have a neck ache. Or a back ache. Or a butt ache. She doesn't eat, she doesn't drink. Nothing. Once she raised up to laugh at his picture on television, but stopped when she realized why she was seeing it there, a funny sick look coming over her face before she slumped down again and went back to sleep.

But she still looks damn good lying there, one leg cocked, hiking her dress up the other. The back of her knee, her thigh, its soft inside. Straight up to that nice bare little cushion of hair. He wants her. Good old Charlene. He'll have her, too. Hell, it may be his last chance for all he knows. He wouldn't want to deny anybody a last chance.

He hopes John Klein had his. Him and his pretty yellow-shorted woman.

They're calling it *brutal. Cold-blooded. Vicious.* It's hard to believe they're talking about him. But it's his face. It's his town. Main Street, the bank, the school, the junkyard. It's his old man coming toward the camera with his hand out, saying something they probably couldn't put on the air. It's him and John Klein in an old shot of the two of them doing a song and dance routine at some party.

He hears what a wonderful person John Klein was, what an credit to his community. He hears about the tennis courts, civic pride, Klein's position in a long-standing family business. He hears about the irony of the first and last Kleins falling victim to bank robberies, the first resulting in a loss that nearly destroyed the bank and, with it, the town, the last resulting in a loss that destroyed the family. John was the only son, the final Klein.

He's sorry about that. He's sorry about a lot of things.

He'd bring him back to life, if he could. He'd go back to bed, if he could, and not get up until it was all over and done with and he was sitting here with Zimmerman drinking beer and saying what a rotten goddamn thing that was to do and he hopes they catch the bastard and string him up.

Senseless, unwarranted, cruel, inhumane.

He hears nothing about himself. *He* doesn't exist. He's a finger that pulled a trigger. He's a specimen in a fishbowl who can see but can't be seen. He's a name and a function to be caught and disposed of.

Last chances only come once.

Why couldn't he have kept his hands off?

Last chances.

He lies next to Charlene on the couch. She's warm. Sleep warm. He puts his arm around her and his leg over her. She stirs but doesn't wake. So warm he could stay there forever.

He backs off when he feels the erection. He doesn't want it now. Not now, coming between them. It's enough just to be there, holding on to her, listening to her sleep.

But he can't help smelling her. Remembering how turned on she was in the car, how she felt through the dress, how nice it is inside her, how she moves.

Just be.

The taste of her skin.

With her.

The sounds she makes when she comes.

Last chance.

Slipping his pants down, he enters her. A sensation so near pain he draws a sharp breath.

She doesn't move.

He finds her breasts and pulls himself against her.

He can't even tell if she's alive, except that she's warm. But there's no stopping now. No stopping. And he wouldn't if he could. Now.

He finishes.

She sleeps. Or pretends to.

He stands beside the couch buckling his belt. He feels like he should pay her.

They've found the car. They even found the nameplate. A garbage collector with a good eye.

Charlene says she's leaving. Back to her mother's. Back to the cowboys. Maybe to an aunt's and uncle's in Texas. Or to a cousin's place she's never seen in Idaho.

"How long do I have?" she wants to know.

They find her at three the next morning, sitting on the front steps of her mother's house, hands folded in her lap like a little girl on her way to Sunday School.

The morning news calls her the "unnamed accomplice," the "mysterious other driver." She at first appears relieved when they lead her handcuffed from the squad car to the lockup. Then she starts, raising her face to the row of cameras, the volley of questions, and peers past them, through them, as if directly at him, tipping forward from the edge of Zimmerman's chair.

He has a silly urge to wave, but doesn't. There's nothing he can do. Now.

In the last shot before the crowd closes behind her, he notices that she has underpants on again.

He can't have long himself. He takes a shower and dresses, expecting to find someone waiting for him in the living room when he goes out. At least it would be over with then. He wouldn't have to think what to do anymore.

But there isn't anyone. There isn't even a lookout outside. The radio says he's still at large.

He can't figure them. They have Charlene, and they must have talked to Zimmerman by now. Haven't they? If they've found him.

And you'd think they would have. Cops can find most anything when they decide they want to.

So why haven't they come? What are they waiting for? Reinforcements? The riot squad to surround the house, some fat bastard out front on a bullhorn telling him to surrender?

He can't picture that. Ronnie Blue just walking out and giving up. Hell, no. He ain't about to. They want him, they'll have to come in after him. And pay the price.

But cops are real chickenshit when you get right down to it. They'll do anything to keep from coming in. Tear gas. Nerve gas. Christ, who knows what? They'll try to flush him out, say he was armed, they fired in self-defense. They'll sneak around back or get him with a sharpshooter from a housetop across the street. At least he saw John Klein's face, talked to him, before he killed him.

To hell with them. He's not about to stay around and be their sitting duck. Not Ronnie Blue. He's busting out. They want him, they'll have to chase him. And he can outdrive and outshoot any of them. Out there. In the open.

He pops the tops on three beers and sets them on the coffee table. Left to right, he chugs them without stopping.

When they're finally there and the two of them—why do they always travel in pairs?—are on their way up the walk, he has to be ready. Perfect timing. Car running, throwing open the garage door, ramming back, knocking them off balance, blasting them with both barrels as they go down. On back into the street, demolishing their car, running the roadblock at the corner. He'll out-maneuver the fuckers all over the city, leaving cops' cars piled up on curbs, storefronts, lawns. Nobody and nothing can touch Ronnie Blue. Not even that last big mother of a barricade on Meridian where he lies in the seat to keep from being hit by broken glass and bullets and puts the throttle to the floor and runs the bastard. Not around it, but right fucking through it. Eighty-five, rubber burning, that motor roaring like some wild animal set loose. Bodies and fenders and boards flying all over. And he comes down on 96 past the interstate, maybe with a wound—blood on his shirt—and a grin, heading north toward the section roads. He knows them all. Where there's dust and no dust. Trench silos, hedgerows, fields out of the way enough to stash a car. They can send out all the helicopters they want and they'll never find him. Not there. Not on his turf. Still at large, they'll be saying until he's so far away nobody'll care. Canada, a ship east to Singapore. He's always wanted to go there. Tahiti, where the women can't hardly wait for you to put it to them. Yes, sir, Ronnie Blue just disappeared and they never did find out where he went to, Ronnie Blue.

22

*N*othing. Nobody. Not a single goddamn sign of
life. Old Gus must even be gone. Or asleep. Or drunk.

He's done everything he can do, waited as long as he can wait.
The car's packed with enough stuff to take him around the world
twice, including Zimmerman's pistol and firecrackers and some of
his clothes. You never know what you might need. Food.

He's washed the dishes, wiped off the kitchen counter and the
coffee table. He's set the trash outside the back door and straightened up the living room. He's flushed the toilet again, just to be
sure.

And he's ready to go. He's ready to hit the road.

Where are they?

On his way out, he opens and relocks the front door from the
inside and double checks the one from the kitchen to the garage.
He doesn't want Zimmerman bitching about the way he left things.

Where the hell are they?

The garage door rolls up. He stands behind his car in full view.
It's like everybody died or moved out overnight or something. Not
even any kids. You always hear kids.

He backs out, closes and locks the garage. He revs the motor, mufflers clattering, and slides on into the street.

At the house next to Gus's the curtain parts. A woman stares out, shaking her head. The curtain closes.

A couple of blocks on another woman is trimming her hedge. In a bathing suit. A green two-piece that looks nice. Real nice. It's a shame he didn't get to know his neighbors better. But maybe it's just as well. They might all have turned out to be like Zimmerman.

There aren't even many cars. One ahead of him, two more approaching, the rest tucked up close to houses like children around their mothers' skirts.

Must be television. Cartoons, game shows, news. Them seeing him inside while he's driving by outside. It's damn near enough to make you laugh.

Traffic on Kellogg is as endless as ever, the lines chopped up by stoplights like hay in a baler. He sees an opening and pulls in.

Not a cop anywhere, people all looking straight ahead, except a couple of kids in a station wagon making faces at him.

At a motel/truckstop just before the by-pass, he sees two patrol cars parked out front. The drivers are inside at a booth by the window. One is smoking a cigarette, the other holding a coffee cup in both hands. The smoker peers out the window, eyes as fixed as a doll's, while Ronnie Blue drives past and out of sight.

Human error. It's no wonder there are so many plane crashes.

But it can't last. Something will break. Something will give. Somebody will look up suddenly one of these times and there he'll be.

Ronnie Blue, how do you do? as he sets it down, burnt rubber piling on their shoes.

Up the ramp and onto the by-pass, he merges beside a couple of girls in a Camaro. They giggle, hands over their mouths. He waves. They practically have orgasms.

It's crazy. It's bizarre.

He leans out his window. "Do you know who I am?"

They turn down the radio, open faces with too much makeup asking him to say it again.

"Do you know who I am?"

"Who?" Braces like a set of miniature railroad tracks on the teeth of the one nearest him.

"Ronnie Blue."

They glance at each other, shrug. "Yeah?"

"I just killed a man."

Frowns. Worry. But no recognition.

"That's not very funny."

The window goes up. They drop behind him, exit at Zoo Boulevard. They'll go back and try again and maybe next time find somebody more to their liking.

He can't believe it. No sirens. No guns. No smell of hot motor oil. It's like he's taking a Sunday drive or something. It's like he's fucking Charlene again.

Hot. Dusty. Section roads all look alike. Hedgerows and wheat stubble and milo, mile after zigzagging mile. Farmers on tractors working the ground, pausing to wipe faces and necks, waving as he passes. Anything to break the rhythm of their jobs and machines. The boredom.

A mile east, a mile north, two east, two north, three east, one south.

It doesn't make any sense. If you traced it out, the route would look like the path of a drunken snake, as his old man used to say.

But he's going generally north, just as he set out to. North and east. Other than that, he hasn't been paying attention. It doesn't really matter. Now. Does it? He'll be where he is when he gets there.

AULNE. No population listed. Because there isn't any. Just a church and graveyard. Son of a bitch. Aulne.

He parks on the shoulder of the road in front of the church, its windows boarded up, eaves rotting, and eats a sandwich and drinks a beer. Warm, but wet. It's ninety-seven, the radio says. Dust covers everything like ashes. But it hasn't hit a hundred yet the way it was supposed to. And it won't. It's too late in the day now.

At large in Aulne.

Even John Klein would laugh, if he heard that. Nobody goes to Aulne. Nothing to go for.

Except the graveyard. He remembers trying to get laid there, but can't remember who he was with. He can't even remember whether he made it. He can see where it was, though. Right behind RUDOLPH SCHMIDT. Right over his face, it would have been, toothy old smile. Why are fucking and dying so much alike? Did John Klein ever bring his Linda woman here? Wouldn't have to really, unless he was doing it for the thrill. Times change, people change. No need to leave the comfort of your own home these days.

Home.

He hopes it was good for them, that they didn't regret it. He wishes they were there now. Home.

Right where he's been going all along. All day. His whole life. Do you ever leave? Can you ever?

He drinks another beer for Rudolph Schmidt and a third for

John Klein, wondering how it is under the ground instead of on top of it.

He pisses in the ditch, shining the weeds and grass, gets in the car and starts back.

23

$\mathcal{S}$itting on the bench under the tower window, he feels like he's about to open a show. Solo. On his own for the first time ever.

RONNIE BLUE APPEARING FOR ONE NIGHT ONLY AT THE FABULOUS KLEIN HOUSE IN BARTLETT'S JUNCTION

People are gathering below, faces he can't really make out in the light, but faces nonetheless, turned up to him the way he's always imagined. Looking up at him, framed with a certain flair, a certain style in the window.

He's tempted to smile and wave. But that might break the spell, the magic moment that usually comes right before a performance.

His old man and his mother aren't there yet. His old man probably won't be, since he's seen him already.

Chester Blue appeared, wrench in hand, from under the hood of a truck he was salvaging, like someone withdrawing from the mouth of a great mechanical beast.

"What're you doing here, you dumb son of a bitch, you stupid bastard? Go on, get on out of here," wrench held up like a club. When he didn't move, his old man turned toward the house: "Ardell, call the goddamn police and tell them the boy's here. Do it. Call them right now."

She wouldn't, of course, not right away, and he stood and looked at his old man until he lowered the wrench and walked off mumbling and swearing.

"Nice seeing you, too," he said and got back in his car and drove to Theophilus Klein's house.

He parked in front and began unloading everything he thought he might need inside. After he'd finished, he closed and locked the window he'd entered by and checked all the rest, making sure their locks were secure and putting whatever he could find—dressers, chairs, sideboards, bookcases—in front of them. He pulled a heavy kitchen cabinet across the back door and an oak table across the cellar door. He made one more round, adjusting this and that. Nobody'd been in the house since he and Charlene had, as far as he could see, and he didn't want them there now. Not unless he knew about it. He didn't want any more surprises, any more interruptions.

He took his things up to the tower window. Charlene's underpants were still on the floor. He picked them up, smelled them, and with a cold knot in his gut—the kind he used to get when he thought he was in love—he folded them and put them on the bench beside him.

And he waited.

Near dusk, Albert Dobbs came out and sat in his porch rocker, neck bowed toward Ronnie Blue's car. For almost a half hour, he peered from the car to the house, sliding forward, leaning back. He finally pushed himself up on the arms of the chair, spit through the railing and went inside.

The big blue Olds floated up to the curb then. Charlie Haskins pulled and humped his fat ass out—any fatter and he'd need a crane—and joined Albert Dobbs on his porch. Charlie sucked on a toothpick and Albert Dobbs folded and unfolded his right arm to point. They could see him, look right at him. But for all he could tell they were talking about the wheat crop, the government, the lack of rain.

They both went inside. In a few minutes Dewey Cole pulled up behind the Olds. He hitched his gun belt and slicked his hair down under his hat.

And they all stared up at him, occasionally pointing, leaning toward one another to hear better. Dewey got back in his car to use his radio.

Other people started coming. Neighbors first, then people they'd called. Cars parking a half block away, doors swinging open, people getting out slowly, like they had the weight of the world on their shoulders. And they clustered together, shaking hands, slapping backs, women and children separating off to nearby porches, men pushing forward, but not too far—all eyes constantly on the window, on him.

"Ronnie Blue, Ronnie Blue," they've been saying softly, nodding. "Ronnie Blue," with respect.

He pushes the window open to hear better. People step back into deeper shadows, the hush settling like night itself.

Talk picks up again with the sound of sirens. The Highway Patrol, the County Sheriff's Patrol.

They use their cars, lights flashing, to seal off the street. Cops crouch behind fenders, pistols and rifles aimed at him.

Cecil Marks, the sheriff, in his Western string tie and Stetson, walks to the middle of the street, carrying a bullhorn. His lips move, but nothing comes out. Someone yells to him. He holds the bullhorn at arm's length as he looks for the button. Finding it, he clears his throat.

"RONNIEBLUE" running his name together the way Carl used to.

He lowers the bullhorn, letting the sound clear, then raises it again, like a cheerleader. But before he can say anything else, he is motioned back to the curb.

Vans with CBS, ABC, NBC painted on them drive up behind the patrol cars. Film crews hurriedly lay their lines and ready their cameras. In each group a man with headphones gets everyone set. One of them goes to where Marks is standing and explains something. Marks nods.

"Get those lights on. The spotlights. On the window there."

He can see it now. A live television special: "The Taking of Ronnie Blue."

Marks lifts the bullhorn.

"CAN YOU HEAR ME RONNIEBLUE"

Stupid bastard.

"COME OUT WITH YOUR HANDS UP"

How do you talk to those things?

"I just want to say—"

"THIS IS THE POLICE COME OUT WITH YOUR HANDS UP"

"I want you to know—"

He sees his mother now, at the edge of the circle of light. Bud and Martha Klein not far away. And Linda.

"—I'm sorry."

"THE HOUSE IS SURROUNDED YOU CAN'T ESCAPE"

Of course no one hears what he says.

"COME OUT"

No one wants to.

Nothing's ever gone together right. Never.

"CAN YOU HEAR ME RONNIEBLUE"

"Can you hear me, Cecil Marks?"

And he'll never have the chance to get it right, either. Now.

"THAT YOU RONNIEBLUE"

"That you, Cecil Marks?"

Marks lowers the bullhorn.

Ronnie Blue rips the paper from a pack of firecrackers. He smiles. He strikes a match.

A nice opening.

"Here's a present for you, Marks."

The firecrackers whizzle and bang and pop.

Wood splinters near his head. Bullets thunk in the stairway behind him.

He lights another pack.

The air fills with smoke and gunpowder.

It's crazy, it's wild, it's beautiful.

He peeks over the window sill. They love it. People running everywhere.

They love him.

The weeds are on fire, a dead evergreen beside the house flaming like a torch. He smells wood smoke.

"Get back. Get back, now. That place is a tinderbox. Somebody get the fire trucks up here."

Son of a bitch.

"COME OUT RONNIEBLUE"

He throws another pack. Another.

The siren sounds at the firehouse. All that commotion. For him.

The truck arrives. He knows everybody on it. They hook up to the hydrant, but the whole front of the house is on fire. He can feel the heat. It's beginning to hurt when he breathes.

"DON'T BE A FOOL BLUE"

Stick it in your ass, Marks.

There's smoke everywhere. A glow beyond the window.

The spotlights are off now, people scurrying back and forth. It's eerie, like a big bonfire, a campfire. Wiener roast. Marshmallows.

Water hisses.

"JUMP BLUE"

He can feel the fire inside. Under his feet. A vaguely satisfying sensation.

"WHAT THE HELL'S WRONG—"

A mistake. A squelch as Marks shuts off the bullhorn.

What will they say?

What will they do?

Will his mother cry?

Will anyone?

God—

When the floor gives way, he isn't sure whether he hears the crackle of flames or applause.